WITCHES' CHILLERS

The harvest moon has risen,

and magick is afoot . . .

There was a crash in the bushes. Cricket's eyes widened. From the exact place she had thrown the dead rabbit, a live one appeared, bursting from the thicket and tearing across the cornfield, full force toward the face of the moon.

Other Books by Silver RavenWolf

Nonfiction
To Ride a Silver Broomstick
To Stir a Magick Cauldron
To Light a Sacred Flame
Teen Witch: Wicca for the New Generation
Angels: Companions in Magick
American Magick: Charms, Spells, & Herbals
Halloween: Customs, Recipes, & Spells

Silver's Spells Series
Silver's Spells for Prosperity
Silver's Spells for Protection
Silver's Spells for Love

Fiction
Beneath a Mountain Moon
Murder at Witches' Bluff

Witches' Chillers Young Adult Fiction Series
Witches' Night Out
Witches' Night of Fear

Kits
Rune Oracle (with Nigel Jackson)
Teen Witch Kit

Visit Silver's website at
http://www.silverravenwolf.com

Witches' Key to Terror

Silver RavenWolf

2001
Llewellyn Publications
St. Paul, MN 55164-0383, USA

This book is a work of fiction. Names, characters, places, and incidents are products of the author's imagination or are used fictitiously. Any resemblance to actual events or locales or persons, living or dead, is entirely coincidental.

First Edition
First Printing, 2001

Cover art ©2001 by Carol Heyer
Cover design by Kevin Brown

Cataloging-in-Publication Data
RavenWolf, Silver, 1956-
   Witches' Key to Terror / Silver RavenWolf—1st ed.
      p.   cm.
   "Witches' Chillers."
   Summary: Sixteen-year-old Cricket enlists the help of the Witches' Night Out coven to help her find the stalker who is threatening her family's farm.

   ISBN 0-7387-0049-5
   [1. Witchcraft—Fiction.   2. Mystery and detective stories.]
I. Title.
PZ7.R19557 Wf2001
[Fic]—dc21

00-067826

Llewellyn Worldwide does not participate in, endorse, or have any authority or responsibility concerning private business transactions between our authors and the public.

   All mail addressed to the author is forwarded but the publisher cannot, unless specifically instructed by the author, give out an address or phone number.

Llewellyn Publications
A Division of Llewellyn Worldwide, Ltd.
P.O. Box 64383, Dept. 0-7387-0049-5
St. Paul, MN 55164-0383
www.llewellyn.com

Printed in the United States of America

*T*his book is dedicated
to those who seek
the magick within.

Chapter 1

Thursday evening, November 17

Sixteen-year-old Cricket Bindart knew that she was in deep trouble, teetering on the edge of certain calamity. The dead bunny dangling from the lip of the mailbox at the end of her driveway was a darned good indication that something was very wrong. The note attached to the limp animal only served as conclusive evidence. "You're fast, but I'm faster," read the black marker scrawled across the paper, "and soon, I'll catch you!" along with a few expletives that her pious father definitely would not appreciate. But who was it for? In the cold moonlight, the animal's blood dripped black across the back of the note, smearing the addressee's name. Was the note for her father? Her older sister? Maybe her twin brother, Tad? Herself? Bile rose in her throat as she quickly wiped her sticky hand on her jeans.

A noise in the orchard to her right made her heart kick into double-time, her breath escaping from her open mouth in rapid puffs. To her left, the light of the full moon trickled across the dead, frost-encrusted stubble of the cornfield. A tendril of autumn-spiced wind fluffed her long, copper hair, splaying the ends across the lifeless form of the bunny. She shuddered, whipping the blood-soaked tresses away with a toss of her head, sending a tiny spatter of red droplets against the hollow mailbox—black tears on moonlit aluminum.

She wasn't sure why she'd stopped at the mailbox at all. Her shift at the family orchard ended late on Thursdays. She was aching, tired, and sweaty. She'd spent the evening loading pumpkins in a wagon for the weekend sale and helping to bottle the last of the fresh cider from the grading shed. Halloween may be over but there were plenty of people around who still kept cold cellars to store apples, potatoes, turnips, and other vegetables. Besides, Thanksgiving was just around the corner. Bindart's Farm and Orchard would be open until after the New Year.

If she ever saw the New Year. She looked at the bloody rabbit again and her bowels turned to water. On examination she realized it wasn't like the bunnies that frequented the farm. The hair was longer, and the animal larger than a wild rabbit. She couldn't quite tell the color of the fur between the blood and the poor lighting, but she thought it might be black. What had her family done to deserve this? And—forget them—what about the poor rabbit? The skin on the back of Cricket's neck itched and she imagined that somewhere in those darkened woods beside the lane someone was watching her. In defiance, she pulled the rabbit free of the mailbox and whipped it into the woods. "I'm not afraid of you!" she shouted. "You think you're tough, don't you, killing a defenseless little bunny! You're scum, that's what you are! Scum!" Her heart pounded and it was all she could do to keep her entire upper body from visibly shaking at the rage and fear screaming inside her.

"What do you think you're doing?"

Cricket spun on her heel, eyes wide. "Tad! You scared the life out of me!"

Her twin brother dipped his blonde head and smirked. "You know, if Dad catches you out here yelling at the moon he'll think you're as batty as our mother."

"Not funny."

Tad shrugged. "What the heck were you doing, anyway?"

Cricket shoved the bloodied paper in her pocket. "Something dead. In the mailbox. I got rid of it but someone will have to hose the mailbox out in the morning."

"Gross. What was it?"

Her eyes skipped over the cornfield, avoiding Tad's questioning gaze. "Some small animal. I didn't bother to look close."

Tad peered at her in the moonlight. "You okay?"

"Yeah. Sure. Why wouldn't I be? I find dead things in our mailbox every day."

Tad glanced over her shoulder at the mailbox.

"Where have you been?" asked Cricket, trying to keep the edge out of her voice. "You were supposed to help me in the grading shed and you never showed up. Then I got stuck loading the pumpkins, which is definitely your job."

Tad smiled mischievously. "Having a good time."

"With whom?"

He shrugged, a habit he did a lot lately. It was as if he didn't care about anything anymore. Not the farm. Not their mother. Not even her. He seemed so distant. Cricket squashed a horrible thought. What if Tad had killed the rabbit and left the note? After all, he had been acting strange lately.

"What's in your pocket?" he asked, stepping forward, his fingers grazing the edge of the crumpled paper, a wisp of a smile on his lips.

"Nothing." She backed off.

He snatched at the paper, catching it deftly in his fingers, his expression switching from playfulness to confusion as he read the note.

"Who wrote this?" he demanded, shaking the paper under her nose.

"As if I know," replied Cricket sarcastically. "Maybe you."

"Me? Why would I do a dumb thing like that?"

It was her turn to shrug. This wasn't the time to get into it.

"Let me get this straight," he said, "you found this note and a dead animal in the mailbox."

She nodded. "A rabbit. Big one. Black, I think."

He turned the note over. "I can't read who it's addressed to."

"Neither can I. Weird, isn't it?"

"Psycho, if you ask me. Who do you think it was for?"

She shook her head while she spoke. "I have no idea."

A crash in the bushes sent them both jumping. From the exact place that she had thrown the dead rabbit, a live one appeared, bursting from the thicket and tearing across the field. They watched the fleet-footed animal meld with the frozen stubble and misty darkness, heading toward the county line, full force toward the face of the moon. Cricket crossed her cold, bloody fists over her heart, her arms blossoming with goosebumps.

Friday, November 18

The white tile walls of the Cedar Crest high-school cafeteria reverberated with the shouts and shrieks of three hundred teens as they did everything but concentrate on first-period lunch. Bethany Salem looked glumly at what was supposed to be pizza. "If I don't get a job soon," she said, picking up the edge of the crust and examining the bottom for strange green growing things, "I'll lose my car. My dad said that he'll cover the insurance, but I've got to come up with the payments or bye-bye Camaro."

"Why did you pick such an expensive car?" asked the ever-practical Tillie Alexander.

Nam Chu peered into her brown lunch bag, slowly extricating a cornucopia of fruits and vegetables, lining them up in a neat row beside the bag.

Tillie finished her pizza and eyed Bethany's plate. "My dad says the same thing, though my car's so old I don't have payments, just repair bills," remarked Tillie as her brown fingers crept close to Bethany's tray. "Are you going to eat that pizza, because if you're not—"

Bethany sighed and pushed the tray toward Tillie. "Go ahead. How you can eat so much and stay rail thin is beyond me." She fanned her hands in disgust.

Tillie grinned, her burnt-almond eyes dancing with pleasure as she snatched the pizza. She'd put psychedelic beads in her cornrows last weekend and they chattered like tiny castanets every time she moved.

"You know," said Bethany, "with your gold-bangle bracelets and tinkling beads, you could pass for a regular symphony."

Tillie sniffed imperiously and ignored the sarcastic comment. "I've got to find a job that lets me have off for cheer practice. We're training for competitions. Most of the jobs around here want you right after school, a no-can-do for me. I've put in a dozen applications, and so far nothing."

Nam's little chin jutted angrily, her blue-black hair swinging against her cheeks. She smashed her brown lunch bag with a delicate fist. "Now that my mother and father have brought so many of our family over from China, there is very little for any of us. I've got to find a job, too! I've looked everywhere. No one's hiring kids."

Tillie frowned. "Nam, you've got the largest wardrobe in Cedar Crest High. Just learn to budget better."

Bethany eyed Nam. Everything Nam wore was always color coordinated and usually top dollar. Today's ensemble consisted entirely of jaunty marigold, from the tips of her shoes to the clips in her hair. It was enough to knock your eyeballs out of your head.

"Why don't you dress like normal people, you know . . . jeans and shirts?" asked Tillie. "You could save a lot of money."

"And look like common rabble, billowing down the hallway in excessive yards of blue denim? I think not," clipped Nam. "I am an individual."

Tillie shot the paper off her straw, aiming at Nam's head.

Bethany snorted. It was obvious that her friends were totally unique, and Bethany loved them for it. Well, most of the time. "You're not running up those credit cards your parents gave you, are you, Nam?"

Nam's emerald eyes shot mental darts at Tillie, as she ignored Bethany's question. "It's a good thing you're my Craft sister," she muttered, then grinned. Her happy expression faded, though, as she turned to Bethany. "Have you seen my gold bracelet? The one with the little charms on it? I've looked everywhere at home and in my locker, but I can't find it. Did I leave it at your house at the last circle meeting?"

Bethany shook her head, her thick, dark hair brushing across her shoulder blades and catching on the back of her sweater. She hated that. "Nope. I sure hope you didn't lose it for good."

Nam pensively bit her lower lip. "It was a present from my father on my sixteenth birthday. He'll be so angry if he thinks I lost it."

Tillie stared into space. "Did you try looking under your bed? I lost my Witches' Night Out necklace and found it mixed with a few dust bunnies under my bed."

"Which reminds me," said Bethany. "Do you think I should have another necklace made at the jeweler in New York, just in case we get a new member in our coven?"

"I think it's the coolest idea that we all share the same necklace," said Nam. "I never take mine off, except when I take a shower. Do you have a new member in mind for the coven?"

"No," said Bethany. "It was just a feeling that came over me last night. Did you look under the bed for your bracelet?"

"Yes, there and just about everywhere else in the house."

"Maybe one of your sisters borrowed it," offered Bethany.

Nam sighed. "I don't think so. My father has very strict rules in our house. It would be a matter of honor and I don't think my sisters would want to face his wrath. He can be a real stickler on that sort of thing."

"Where's Sidney?" asked Tillie. "I haven't seen him all day."

Bethany smiled dreamily. Of German and Native American extraction, Sidney Bluefeather was the fourth member of Bethany's coven, dedicated only a few weeks ago. He also set her heart on fire.

"Hel-lo? Earth to Bethany," laughed Tillie.

Bethany grew serious. "Um, I've been meaning to tell you about that. Sidney and his mother drove his stepsister into New York City today."

Nam stopped examining a carrot, looking up in surprise. "You mean Gillian?"

"Yes. Gillian was accepted into a great art school. She'll finish out her regular high-school curriculum there. His mother wants to do a regular sight-seeing extravaganza. He's not supposed to be back until after Thanksgiving," she added glumly.

"Gillian's gone?" asked Tillie, slurping her milk. "Every time we get someone new in the group, they leave. That's three in two months."

Bethany sighed. "Group work isn't for everyone. The ones that left are still practicing, but they're living in other places now, like Gillian."

"I didn't realize working with a group would be so hard," grumbled Tillie. "You just get used to someone, and then they split."

"Think you can hang on until Sidney comes home?" teased Nam, making smacking sounds with her gold-glossed lips. "You've been dating . . . what? A few weeks? What sort of kisser is he?"

Bethany shot her a vicious look. "I wouldn't know. I want to take the relationship nice and easy. I'll be just fine, thank you very much!"

Someone in the cafeteria shrieked and the whole place broke into pandemonium. Kids jumped on chairs, some threw trays in surprise, while one of the lunch ladies did an awkward pirouette and fell headfirst into a pan of pizza.

"What's going on?" shouted Tillie.

"An animal," screamed someone. "No! A dozen of them! Amazonian rabbits from Mars loose in the cafeteria!" More squeals as some students dove to catch the furry creatures. Live bunnies ricocheted off walls, flew past chairs, and scurried under tables. "Senior prank!" screamed one of the cheerleaders. "Run for your lives!"

One black rabbit skittered down Bethany's table, his whiskers trembling with curiosity. He stood on his hind legs, staring right at her. She looked at the rabbit in disbelief. Tillie made a grab for it but the rabbit was too quick for her. The black bunny snatched a lone carrot by Nam's lunch bag.

"Thief! Pirate! Vagabond!" shrilled Nam.

"Someone in the agricultural class must have brought them in here and let them go," Tillie said, laughing so hard she couldn't stand up straight. "You ever see a black rabbit before? I mean, I thought most of them were brown, or gray . . . even white."

Bethany shrugged, righting a spilled milk carton and sopping up the mess with napkins. "They breed exotic ones in the agricultural department. Sidney took me down there once. They even have a pair of chinchilla rabbits. Somebody's gonna be upset. Those rabbits are expensive to keep and are probably someone's project for the year. I hope they can catch them all without hurting them."

The warning bell rang, signaling ten minutes to their next class. The girls gathered up their trash, flowing easily along with the lunch mob, still excited from the attack of the dreaded Cedar Crest rabbits.

"I've been working on a spell to get a good job," said Bethany as the girls left the cafeteria. "So far, though, nothing's happened. Ramona says that I have to get out and look for a job, that magick won't just bring one to me. I don't understand why I can't just snap my fingers and get one! What good is studying magick for months on end if it doesn't provide instantaneous results? Sometimes I wonder why we study Witchcraft all! I get so frustrated! There's just as much book work as in school and we don't seem to be getting very far. I mean, it's not like on television. Those Witches get to snap their fingers and ta-da! It's disgusting."

"We should be so lucky," sighed Nam.

Tillie chuckled. "I can hear Ramona now . . . *ma cherie, nothing will come to you unless you work for it . . . you must have patience and practice, practice, practice*," she mimicked and dropped her voice, "*and remember . . . be careful what you wish for!*" She wiggled her fingers in front of her nose, her gold bracelets jingling merrily. "You've got to admit, your Hoodoo housekeeper is a major hoot!"

Nam laughed. "How about this?" She snapped her fingers in the air in the shape of a star and said, "Power near and power far, I wish upon a magick star! We three need jobs, and need them soon, lovely Lady of the Moon!"

Tillie rolled her eyes. "Oh, please . . . as if that will work! If I don't get moving, I'm going to be late for English Lit."

"Nice try, Nam," said Bethany, "but I think there's more to it than that."

Nam pouted. "Wait up," she said as she hurried after them. They cruised through the sea of kids toward the sophomore bank of puke-pink lockers. "Hold it," she said. "I have to stop and get my lit book."

The girls gathered around Nam as she tried to rummage through her locker and still hang onto the edge of her yellow stretch miniskirt crawling stubbornly up her thighs.

"It would be nice if we could all find a job where we could work together," said Tillie.

Janet Atkins, stowing her books in a locker a few doors down, turned to look at the three girls, brushing a curtain of dark hair away from her Mississippi eyes. "Did I hear you say you wanted a job?" she asked, her voice like honey dripping off the edge of a switchblade.

Tillie nodded suspiciously.

"Well!" said Janet, banging her locker shut. "Bindart's Orchard is looking for some help." She adjusted her Coach leather purse on her shoulder. "But I warn you, people quit almost as soon as they're hired."

"Where's Bindart's Orchard?" mumbled Nam as she squatted on the floor, madly pawing through the contents at the bottom of her locker, modesty temporarily forgotten.

Janet cast kohl-lined eyes down the hall, as if she expected someone to overhear her. "It's by the county line. Not far. Northern territory."

"Oh," said Tillie.

"Northern High," said Nam, her voice muffled by the locker. She popped out, tilting her head upwards, blinking rapidly. "That's our rival school. No kid from Cedar Crest in their right mind ever goes there. Bunch of rednecks and farm kids. Rough place. Anyone that would work in that county is an idiot." That said, she ducked her head back in the locker.

"Chicken," said Tillie, turning her attention back to Janet. "How do you know everyone quits that works there?"

Janet moved her rosebud lips as if weighing how much she should say. "Because I just quit."

"Open mouth, insert foot," muttered Bethany, looking at Nam's wiggling backside as she continued to forage in her locker.

Janet ignored the slur. "You can certainly have my job. The place is haunted."

"Get out!" said Tillie, the beads in her hair clicking as she shook her head in disbelief. "That's ridiculous."

Janet tossed her head, her smile this side of coquettish. "I swear it's the truth. I won't step foot on that property, and I wouldn't recommend it to just anyone." She lowered her voice. "Besides, the family that owns the orchard is weird. The twins are home-schooled and the parents don't like the help mixing with their kids for fear our progressive ways will rub off on them. There's an older sister, in her thirties, and she's as straight-laced as they come. Ever since the fire two years ago, she carries a shotgun around with her like a pocketbook. The mother doesn't speak a word. Not to anyone. Not even her own children. The place reminds me of a horror novel or something." She squared her slender shoulders. "Me? I wouldn't go back there for twice the salary."

"Fire?" asked Bethany. "What fire?"

"Dunno," replied Janet, "I wasn't around. Talk I heard at the orchard. You know."

"No, I don't know," replied Bethany, staring at Janet. Somehow she felt the girl was lying. Maybe about the jobs, or the fire, or all of it.

Tillie pawed through her purse and produced a pack of crackers. "So, what scared you so bad you don't want to go back?"

Janet opened her mouth, then snapped it shut, gritting her teeth. She took another breath, and said, "I'd rather not say."

Bethany spoke. "If you won't say, and wouldn't send any of your friends there for a job, then why would you tell us to go there?"

A furtive grin spread across Janet's fine-boned face. "Perhaps a challenge?" She looked pointedly at Bethany. "Or maybe because everyone in the school knows you three are Witches. I'm sure that place would be right down your alley. Like I said, there was a terrible fire two years ago. The kids' mother hasn't spoken a word since then. Runs around the place like some kind of wildcat. There's supposed to be a ghost, too. I never saw it, but some of the migrant workers claim it haunts the butterfly garden. Then some woman, another worker, disappeared last summer. The place is full of freaks. You all being Witches, well, you get my drift." She smirked, flipping her dark hair over her shoulder. "I'm thinking of transferring to Northern, you know. They have a much better debate team and the school is larger. Those rednecks, as you call them, have a lot to offer a pretty girl like me." She sashayed down the hall, her slender hips swaying. "Besides, I don't think they have any Witches."

Nam straightened, slamming the locker shut. "She's not pretty. Her face looks like a horse pooped on it."

"Creep," muttered Tillie. "She's on my debate team, that's why she said that. Used to be a friend of Vanessa's. Can't stand her. She's a senior. I was glad she's graduating this year. I hope she does transfer. No one on the team likes her. She's doesn't like underclassmen, and she specifically hates sophomores."

"And that would be us," said Bethany.

Nam looked at Janet's retreating figure. "Aw, don't listen to Janet. She's not so bad. It's those self-serving preps she hangs out with. I've talked to her lots of times. When she's alone, she's just fine."

Bethany bowed her head. "Let me get this straight. You just made a nasty comment about her face, and now you're saying she's not so bad. I don't understand you."

"Never listen to a Libra," said Tillie, smiling at Nam. "They're so busy being fair they always get screwed."

Nam dilated her little nostrils. "Better than a Leo!"

Tillie stuck her hand on her hip. "I'll have you know that Leos are the courageous ones of the zodiac! So what if we want to show off now and then!"

Bethany broke in. "Yeah, and if given the chance, you'll throw all of us off the stage."

Tillie sniffed, extending her hand in a queenly manner. "Far better than your Scorpio sensibilities that can't take a joke."

Bethany held up her hands in mock defense. "If we don't get moving, we'll be in detention. English literature and *Beowulf* calls."

"Black rabbits," muttered Tillie. "I wonder how they got out?"

"Forget the rabbits," said Nam. "What do you think we ought to do about getting jobs?"

"Not being one to back down from a challenge," answered Bethany, a furtive grin flitting across her face, "I think we should go for it. Visit Bindart's. How about you?"

"To Bindart's!" shouted Tillie.

"To *Beowulf*," squealed Nam.

The bell rang.

"To detention," muttered Bethany.

Chapter 2

Friday evening

Cricket sat at the gray formica kitchen table, shivering. Why did it always have to be so drafty in this house? The bare bulbs from the light fixture hanging overhead hurt her eyes. Tad broke the glass shade last summer and her father refused to buy a new one; now everyone in the house had to suffer, but no one dared say anything. She shoved her schoolbooks forward and slumped in the chair. She swore she did more homework than any kid at public school. Hour upon hour and always after a long day in the orchard. She rubbed a stiff spot on the back of her neck, wishing she had a different life than this one.

Tad stomped through the kitchen, his face blank, which meant he was hiding something. Cricket glanced at the clock on the stove. "Past eleven again. You better watch it, Tad. One of these days Dad is going to figure out you're not working in the orchard and then there's going to be hell to pay."

Tad opened the refrigerator door and pulled out the half-empty milk jug, making no comment.

"I had to cover for you again," Cricket said, knowing she sounded like a whining female. "Don't you dare!" she exclaimed as he lifted the jug to drink from it. "Get a glass. You'd think you were raised in a barn!"

He shrugged, took a glass tumbler from the drain board and filled it with milk. He did not, however, reply to her accusation. "Where's Dad?"

"He took a load of cider to Dwyers' Market. He should be back a little after midnight. Leslee went to Shippensburg to check on new equipment, and Momma is in her room, as usual, watching her westerns. She's probably asleep by now." Cricket slapped her biology book shut with a resounding thwap. "I can't keep covering for you, Tad. I'm already three chapters behind in biology, and three in social studies. I realize that Dad keeps a tight rein on us, and I don't mind you disappearing now and then, but it's too often. Sooner or later he's going to catch you, and if I'm this far behind on my studies, you must really be backlogged."

Tad pulled out a chair and sat across from her.

"Does it strike you funny that Leslee takes an awful lot of overnight trips lately?" asked Cricket.

"I don't know. Leslee never says much. If she's found a way to get out from under Dad's thumb, then more power to her. I can't believe she didn't just stay in the service. At least you get half-decent pay for somebody ordering you around. I am so sick of this place. It's cold in winter, hot in the summer. My bed is twenty years old and hurts my back.

We don't even have a microwave. Our clothes look like they came from some museum auction. This house sucks. Our lives suck. And to top it off, there wasn't one rabbit, there were two," finished Tad.

"Two?" Cricket's eyes grew wide.

"And you don't want to know what happened to the second one. I found it out by the front gate this morning." He held up his hand. "No note. They were chinchilla rabbits. I saw some at the Farm Show in Harrisburg last January. Big, expensive. You don't just find them in the field."

"Do we know anyone that has rabbits like that?"

He shook his head. "No, but I'm asking around. Somebody's got to know something."

"You know," said Cricket, pausing to chew on her lip, "I'm hearing rumors."

Tad put his head back and closed his eyes. "Yeah? Like what? We have more rumors than fruit at this stupid farm."

Cricket traced the outline of the Siberian tigers on the front of her bio book. "Like you've been messing around with some of the local girls."

"Where'd you hear that?"

"The only person people don't talk to around here is Dad. Gossip is the prime source of amusement. Especially for the migrant workers."

"As if I care," he replied, eyes still closed.

She ignored his comment. "Is it true? About the girls?"

"And if it is?"

"Don't get in trouble."

He opened one eye, a grin tugging at his lips. "Are you trying to lecture me on the birds and the bees?"

"Not only is this an orchard, it is also a farm. We learned about the birds and the bees when we were six and helped Dad birth that foal. Yes, that's part of what I mean, but not the whole of it. Things can get out of hand. People can get hurt. Most times girls assume you love them if you want to have sex. If they think they've been deceived, things can mushroom."

Tad opened both eyes and sat up straight. "As if you're the expert."

She blushed. Her father watched her far more than Tad, telling her point-blank that she would have to wait until she was eighteen to date. At sixteen she felt like she was under a death sentence. "Just because I can't participate doesn't mean I don't watch. You could get into a lot of trouble, Tad. Some of those Northern boys aren't going to like it if you are messing with their sisters, especially if you are running more than one at a time."

"I'm glad you care," he said sarcastically.

Her shoulders slumped. Her brother used to be so kind. They'd spent every waking moment of their childhood together. Growing up meant growing apart. She didn't like it. Cricket sighed, then said, "Look, Tad, I'm not just trying to be nosy. That note could have been for you."

He snorted.

"I mean it. What if it's from some girl's brother?"

"It's probably for Dad. He's a nasty old fart. Nobody around here likes him."

"Then they would have done something about it before," said Cricket. "This has to do with something recent. Must be."

"Maybe it was for Leslee," volunteered Tad. "She scares the crap out of a lot of people with that shot-gun of hers. Maybe she waved it at someone once too often?"

Cricket shivered. "I don't think so. Once most people get to know Leslee, they really like her."

Tad leaned forward. "Maybe it was Martha Owens."

"Now you're being stupid," replied Cricket. "Why would Martha have left a thing like that? Besides, she's been gone since summer."

"She used to burn all them saint candles, and once I remember how everybody said she got one of the other workers out of jail by making a petition to some saint—Barbara, I think. Everybody around here was talking about it."

"What does burning a candle and writing some words on a piece of paper—which is what a petition is, you dope—have to do with a mutilated rabbit? Besides, Dad said she went out west, down to New Mexico or Texas. I forget exactly where."

"That's just it," said Tad. "Nobody knows where she went. She didn't even collect her last two weeks' pay."

"How do you know that?"

"I saw the check stuck in the back of one of Dad's ledgers a few months ago. He said she never came and got it, and he doesn't know where to send it."

"That's odd," murmured Cricket. "That's not what he told me."

Tad warmed to the topic. "That's what I said, that it was odd." He raised his sandy eyebrows and widened his blue eyes, nodding his head. "But Dad claimed that it's normal for migrant workers to just disappear. He said they do it all the time. They find a better farm and off they go."

"But Martha was with us for fifteen years."

Tad slapped the table. "I said the same."

"He told me she found a better job," said Cricket doubtfully. "Why would he lie to me like that?"

"He probably just didn't want you to worry," said Tad, rising from the table. "We got any cookies around here?"

"She's been gone since summer," mused Cricket. "Even if she was around here, at another farm, I mean, she would never have hurt anything, not even a rabbit." She shook her head. "No, it wasn't Martha, I'm sure of it."

"Then who?" asked Tad, pawing through the kitchen cupboards.

"That's what I'm asking you. If you're doing anything you shouldn't, Tad, you better be careful."

"We lost another five workers today," he said glumly. "If this keeps up we'll be out of business before Christmas."

"I just don't understand it," said Cricket.

"The workers are superstitious," replied Tad. "Someone is telling them that the orchard is haunted. One guy in the group today told me he heard fiddle music in the garden late last night."

"What? We've got to find out who is spreading these rumors!"

"Even if we do, it's probably too late to do anything about it." Tad picked up her American Government studies book and started to leaf through it. "What's this?" he asked, pulling out a newspaper clipping stuffed between the pages.

Cricket groaned inwardly as Tad read the headline aloud, "'Cedar Crest Witches Crack New York City Double-Homicide Case.' What is this shit?"

"Some girls over in Cedar Crest helped the police," she replied nonchalantly.

"Witches? Spare me. You don't believe in that junk, do you? Why did you cut this out?"

"Local interest. Schoolwork."

Tad laughed. "Oh, yeah, like Dad would like that. He'd have heart failure if he knew you saw this, much less believed in it. This stuff is the reason why he won't let us attend public school. Nuts like those girls." His expression soured as he tossed the clipping back to her. "If they kept the weirdos out of the school system, kids like us could go."

"You act like you know them," said Cricket suspiciously.

"Heard of them. That was enough. They're freaks. You'll never catch anyone like that around here, that's for sure. Dad would have a cow."

"You three look like a trio of cats sitting on a fence rail," huffed Ramona as the housekeeper bustled around the warm Salem family kitchen shaking a wooden spoon at them. "To me, that means trouble is brewing. Ramona saw three ravens strutting in her garden this afternoon. And, O Great Mother, there was a *lapin noire!*" She made the sign of the cross over her billowing white blouse. "Ramona must light a candle!"

The three girls milled around the kitchen, dodging Ramona, looking for midnight snacks. Bethany wished for the thousandth time that the housekeeper would not talk about herself in the third person. Too weird.

"What's a *lapin noire*?" asked Nam, nosing in the vegetable drawer of the refrigerator.

"A black rabbit," answered Ramona. "Sent by the Lady herself, I am sure."

Bethany turned away to hide her amusement. Ramona thought there was a message in everything, even when she found a spider in the toilet.

"Black rabbit?" asked Tillie. "You saw a black rabbit in the garden. Did he say anything to you?"

Nam lightly punched her. "This isn't Alice in Wonderland and, unless the rabbit had on a hat, I think we can safely assume he only knows bunny language. Probably an escapee from the Cedar Crest Ag room."

Bethany sniggered.

Her cat, Hecate, slithered into the kitchen, nose to the ground, whiskers vibrating.

Ramona snorted with indignation. "Ma cherie! It was a message from the spirits. I'm sure of it." She turned back to the stove, muttering over a large pot of vegetable soup that filled the kitchen with a mouth-watering aroma. "Ramona is positive something's in the air. A message of some sort." She shivered. "And not just the superb essence of my cooking!" She looked down at the cat. "The back door was open and Hecate took after it like his tail was on fire! Silly kitty!"

Hecate flattened his ears and hissed.

Ramona threw a bit of meat in his dish. "Here you go, brave one, this piece of meat ought not to be too quick for you."

Hecate glared at her, then stalked over to his dish.

"Why are you cooking vegetable soup at midnight?"

"It's for the firemen."

"Oh, that's right," said Tillie, hovering near the pot. "What would those guys do down at the firehouse if you missed a Saturday?"

"Starve," said Ramona matter-of-factly. "They don't eat so good. Now! You girls have been twittering all evening. What's going on?"

"We got jobs," Bethany said. "We're all going to work at Bindart's Orchard, at least until Christmas."

Ramona clucked her tongue, placing a large platter of cookies in the center of the table.

"That's right," said Tillie. "We went out there after school and the guy that owns the orchard hired us on the spot! The only bad thing is that we won't all be working together at the same place or at the same time."

Nam flounced down at the kitchen table, her little mouth crunching on a piece of celery. She waved the celery stalk at the other girls. "I don't know about you guys, but I thought old Mr. Bindart was as weird as Janet said, and I thought that girl from Northern in the store was strange, too. What's her name? Alice Clement?"

"That's her, all right. I didn't think Bindart was so bad. Geez, Nam, you're not usually so judgmental. What gives?"

"I don't know. Just a feeling, I guess. Something's definitely wrong with that guy."

Tillie pulled out a chair and sat opposite Nam, drumming her fingers on the red tablecloth, the gold bracelets on her arm clanking. "You were ready to believe what Janet told you before you got there, that's all. I thought the whole setup was quaint. Cute little store. All those beautiful mums around, and that great produce. The tan paint on all the buildings with dark brown trim. Neat place. Don't let your imagination run away with you. You just didn't like that girl in the store because she was from Northern." Her fingers danced across the tablecloth and snatched one of Ramona's famous chocolate cookies.

Nam pursed her gold-slicked lips and shook her head, pointing the celery stalk at Tillie. "It's more than that."

Ramona looked at the trio seriously. "One's gut feelings are usually correct. If Nam says that she doesn't feel right about the orchard, perhaps you should not work there." Bethany joined the girls at the table. "Hey, I don't care how strange any of them are. I need the money. My car payment is due soon and I've pretty much depleted my savings since I lost my job at the diner."

"She's right," said Nam, looking apologetically at Ramona. "It's probably nothing. Not a gut feeling at all. Just my imagination. I can't afford not to work and I've put in applications all over town. Bindart's is the only place that would hire me."

Bethany turned to the housekeeper. "Did Dad leave for Los Angeles okay?"

Ramona nodded, her white-scarved head bobbing. "He said for you to be good and he will see you in two weeks."

"He's lucky," said Bethany. "He gets to go to a homicide conference in California and I have to stay here. Yuck!"

"Cut him a break," said Tillie. "He works hard at the NYPD. Maybe a little sun and fun will do him some good."

"Yeah," remarked Nam. "Fun talking about murder cases. How exciting." She wrinkled her nose. "Did either of you see the Bindart twins?"

Both girls shook their heads. Nam said, "I saw Janet after school. She told me that the twins are our age and reminded me they're home-schooled. I don't think I'd like that. I mean, how would you meet kids your own age? Anyway, she said they work out there most days and weekends, unless there's a big push on a particular produce, then they work at night, too."

"Yeah," said Tillie, "but think of the bright side. Study at your own pace. No rushing to classes and forgetting your stuff. No grumpy teachers. No having to deal with bullies, or being embarrassed because you don't have money for the hottest styles . . . you wouldn't have to get up every morning and stand outside in the cold waiting for the bus, either." She bit into a cookie, her expression thoughtful.

"No cheerleading," remarked Nam.

"Bummer," said Tillie.

"No debate team," added Bethany.

"Hmmm," replied Tillie.

"No swimming in the school pool," reminded Ramona.

"Forget that!" said Tillie.

"I didn't see anyone but that Alice girl in the store," mused Bethany. "I wonder what the twins are like?"

Nam's emerald eyes took on that knowing, gossipy look. "Janet says they aren't allowed to socialize with the hired help because the parents think that we'll introduce them to devil worship, rock music, and—dare I say it?—sex!" She laughed. "And here's the worst part . . . " she leaned over the table, her eyes widening in horror, "their mother makes all their clothes!" Nam shook her head sadly on that one. "Surely this is a fate worse than death."

"Sounds like a prison environment to me," said Tillie. "Don't they have any friends?"

Nam examined her gold nail polish, picking a small chip off her index finger. "Not the girl, but Janet says that the boy has a secret girlfriend."

"How does she know that?" asked Tillie.

"Beats me," replied Nam.

Saturday, November 19

One thing was for absolute sure—Bethany hated Alice Clement, the little blonde bigmouth at the Bindart Orchard store. Alice was nastier than an alligator with a toothache. For the past four hours of this otherwise pleasant Saturday morning, Alice made it her business to screech orders at Bethany, not lifting so much as a pudgy finger to do anything herself.

Bethany wiped the gritty sweat off her forehead and, broom in hand, proceeded to sweep the wide front porch of the store. She could feel Alice's eyes raking her back but she was determined not to let the girl get her fired from her first day on the job. What was this girl's problem, anyway?

Bethany reached for the dustpan to pick up a few scraps of trash but before she could grab the handle, Alice kicked the pan away from Bethany's fingers. Bethany rose, a vein angrily throbbing in her temple, creating a tingling sensation in her ears. "You didn't have to do that," said Bethany quietly between immovable teeth, trying her best to control her emotions. *Well-trained Witches bend like a willow*, at least that's what Ramona said. Bethany took a deep breath. Although unacceptable, part of her truly wanted to kick this girl's face in.

Alice's gray-green eyes flicked over the parking lot.

No one in sight, thought Bethany, *here it comes*.

"We don't need people like you here."

Oh, boy.

"I can handle the store just fine." Alice leaned against the door frame and crossed well-muscled arms. The morning sun splayed mottled patches of white light on her close-cropped blonde hair, her gelled bangs glistening in spiky wisps. Bethany seriously wondered if the girl was demented.

"I like it here," said Bethany, "and I'm not planning to quit anytime soon."

"We'll see about that," hissed Alice, her chin raised in defiance.

Bethany retrieved the dustpan and continued sweeping. Some big guy with a full, dark beard emerged from the grading shed across the parking lot and lumbered toward the equipment shed. Head down, he didn't even look in their direction. A dirty red bandanna flapped around his thick neck.

The last of the golden yellow and blood-red leaves swarmed over the porch in a gust of wind. Bethany sighed. More sweeping.

"I couldn't believe it when Old Man Bindart said he hired Cedar Crest sluts," said Alice, playing her fingers above the elbow of her crossed arms. "And just about dropped dead when I found out it was Witch trash."

"Too bad you didn't," muttered Bethany as she continued sweeping.

"Janet Atkins told me all about you people. She stopped by my house last night."

Bethany contemplated this piece of news. It sounded like Janet was trying to set them up. Maybe Nam was right. There was something rotten about this place, and it was probably this girl. She eyed Alice. Pretty soon she just might take this broom and clobber Alice with it. The image made her think of Ramona, and she smiled, letting go of her anger. *No wonder Janet quit,* thought Bethany, *if she had to deal with Alice the Malice every day,* but that didn't make sense. Not if Janet made a special effort to stop and see the girl last night. Well, it wasn't worth wasting good brain cells over.

Although Bethany ignored her, Alice didn't appear to be moving anytime soon. Bethany walked down the wooden steps, clearing away bits of grass, leaves, and dirt. She could feel Alice's eyes trying to mentally slice her into ribbons. What made people like her so mean was a mystery to Bethany, though Ramona always told her that cruelty has a root—a reason—and it takes a strong person to unearth that long tendril of pain before the individual could be kind again. *Evil grows if left unchecked,* preached Ramona. If that was so, then this girl had a whole garden of it.

Another puff of wind blew around the collar of Bethany's blue sweater. She shivered. In a few days, the last of the Mother's autumn attire would be chopped and mulched, rotting atop barren vegetable gardens all over the county. Just one more storm and the empty tree limbs would be clawing at the muzzy November sky.

As the broom swung for a final swish on the bottom step, Bethany noticed an odd ball of wire stuck under the corner of the step. She reached down to move it, but quickly snatched her hand away. A piece of paper fluttered from one of the biting barbs. A tanglefoot!

"What are you looking at?" asked Alice coldly, moving to the top step to survey the area below.

"Just a piece of junk," replied Bethany, trying to keep her voice calm.

"Get it cleaned up," barked Alice. "We've got jams and jellies to set out and I'm not carrying those heavy boxes. You can do it. I get enough exercise at the gym."

Bethany ignored Alice, her thoughts whirling like confetti thrown at a fan. Who would put such a nasty charm here? The tanglefoot was a simple piece of folk magick, and this little monstrosity was geared for cruel intentions—to make sure those residing within the dwelling met with continued obstacles so that their life path turned into one tripping sensation after another. Questions ripped through Bethany's mind in rapid-fire succession.

Who was the tanglefoot meant for?

Why would someone put it by a business?

Worse: was there someone working at Bindart's skilled in negative magick? She nudged the tanglefoot with the bristles of the broom. The evil little thing seemed to sparkle in the sunlight as it rolled under the step, but really it was gray and dirty. A trick of the light? Bethany stood straight, rolling her shoulders to relieve the tension. Her eyes flicked over the environment. The countryside was quiet. Peaceful. On the horizon, the lip of South Mountain blended like a soft pastel painting into the blue-gray sky above.

Did the Bindarts practice magick? No. They home-schooled, for religious reasons most likely, and only a few pagans across the country actually did that. Most of the home-school kids were the straight-laced kind. Besides, no one would negatively magick themselves. That would be stupid. An employee, perhaps? Huh. Well, she'd soon find out. Magickal people usually recognized one another, even if it was only on a subconscious level, and those who worked negative magick had every right to fear the strength of the positive Witch. Bethany would have to keep her eyes open and warn Nam and Tillie.

Bethany looked up to scrutinize Alice, but the girl disappeared into the store. Was Alice the culprit? Cruel—yes; magickal? Probably not. Bethany walked cautiously back up the stairs, peering in through the front door. Alice's back was turned as she busily spoke to a customer.

Bethany allowed her eyes to defocus a bit. Alice looked, well . . . too doughy, like her aura was soft and mushy, not bright and sparkling nor black and hateful. It was then that Bethany realized Alice's behavior was only a front. It was too bad the girl was uncomfortable with the self inside, and chose, instead, to hide her true being behind poisoned words. Bethany contemplated whether Alice was of the salvageable variety or should best be left alone.

Bethany slipped back down the steps. Using the broom, she moved the tanglefoot back into the light, better to see what was written on the paper. Without touching the wire, she balanced on her haunches to look at it closer. For a second her imagination carried her away and she thought the ball of wire might jump up on its own and bite her. She laughed nervously, thinking, *Don't be silly. It isn't even meant for me.* She poked at it with the broom handle until the paper was visible. Only one name, printed in black ink—Bindart. Looking closer, she saw a nest of herbs and dirt wadded in the center. She shivered.

An unholy shriek from the grading shed snapped her head back, her eyes riveted to the converted garage. By the second scream she was halfway across the parking lot, heading toward the grading shed at a dead run. Alice, out the door like a shot from a muzzleloader, pounded behind Bethany, her meaty arms moving at piston pace.

Chapter 3

Bethany rushed into the shed, blinking rapidly, willing her sun-constricted pupils to adjust in the artificial lighting. She could feel Alice huffing at her back but didn't turn, propelled forward by the hysterical babbling within. The grading shed appeared to be nothing more than a windowless, modernized garage outfitted with several large, flat tables currently heaped with the last of the prize-winning Bindart apples. The rest of the shed was filled with a small conveyer belt, heavily stocked shelves of canned fruit, the cider machine in the far corner, and hundreds of wooden crates piled against the walls.

The girls weren't the only ones to hear the screams. Old Man Bindart flew through the door, pushing past Bethany, followed by the husky fellow with the black beard and blue-jean coveralls she'd seen earlier. A teenage boy stood by the conveyor belt, a puddle of blood at his feet, shocked horror in his blue eyes. Blood streamed from his outstretched hand, yet the teen only stared at a lone finger, perched precariously on top of a pile of apples. Nam, eyes wide, stood with her back pressed to the wall, mouth agape in horror. The unintelligible shrieks must have come from her. Clad entirely in green, she looked like a shaking elf with sweaty, blue-black hair.

Clarence, the man who'd actually hired them and the only other employee in the shed, was frantically searching for something to tie off the stub of the boy's finger. Blood jetted everywhere in rhythmic spatters—the floor, the walls, the cider machine, and the apples. The burly fellow offered his bandanna while Old Man Bindart shouted for Alice to get a bag of ice out of the freezer next door. Nam, galvanized by the entrance of the adults, raced across the parking lot to call emergency services. And still, the boy remained mute.

"I can't get the blood to stop!" cried Clarence, his ancient face paralyzed with concern as he worked the bandanna.

Bethany knew what to do, but she wasn't sure if she should say anything or not. A girl her age rushed into the shed, long red hair stuck in sweated clumps to her forehead, a homespun shirt wet from the exertion of running clinging to her slender frame. Bethany looked at her sunburned face devoid of makeup, unnaturally blue eyes wild with fear. "Oh, my God!" the girl screamed. "Tad!" These two young strangers must be the Bindart twins.

Old Man Bindart stepped forward and shoved the girl back out the door. "Go tell your mama there's been an accident," he said quietly. "Take the golf cart." The girl hesitated, then turned and bolted toward the little cart still idling by the door where Old Man Bindart must have left it.

The injured boy fainted and slumped to the cold concrete floor.

"I think I could help," squeaked Bethany, her voice sticking in her throat. This was the first time in her life she was about to tell perfect strangers, especially adults, that she was different, that she had an unusual skill . . . she swallowed hard. "I know how to stop blood."

All three men looked at her like she was crazy.

"Get her out of here," rumbled Bindart. The big guy, she thought she heard someone call him Zee, stepped toward her.

Bethany tensed her shoulders. "We're on the edge of the county line. It'll take twenty minutes before the emergency people come. He could die before then. Let me at least try. I don't even have to touch him," she pleaded.

Clarence cocked his old head. A foot smaller than Bethany and at least sixty years her senior, he looked her square in the eyes. "There ain't nobody around here in over thirty years that could stop blood, 'cept Grandpa Bindart and maybe Martha Owens, but they're gone." He looked desperately at the boy. "But if you think you can do it . . ."

"I can at least try," said Bethany, her voice quavering. She could feel her stomach knotting in fear. What if she failed?

Old Man Bindart growled, his face showing that he was clearly torn between throwing her out and letting her help his son. Finally, he said nothing, stepping out of her way. *For some reason,* Bethany thought, *Clarence must carry weight with Bindart, but now's not the time to think about it.*

Bethany carefully stepped over most of the blood and leaned close to Tad. The boy's breathing was shallow and erratic, his skin deadly white, fading to blue. She held her hands, palms outstretched over his injury, watching the blood rush through the bandanna like juice through a sieve. "The bandanna isn't tight enough," she said through clenched teeth. If she opened her mouth, she might empty the contents of her lunch on the frigid concrete floor.

Hands fumbled at the knots.

"Does anyone have a black marker?" she asked.

"What? This girl is nuts!" said Zee.

Bethany, eyes blazing, stared him down. "Look, you have to write the time you put the bandanna on his hand in black marker on his forehead. Once he gets to the hospital, they only have so many minutes to take care of him or he'll lose the rest of his finger, maybe his life! This way the emergency doctors can't miss the time! And get that finger on ice!"

Someone scrambled for a marker while a gruff male voice demanded to know what was keeping Alice.

Her hands trembled but she bit her lip and took a deep breath, closed her eyes, and summoned the power within. "Holy Mary, Mother of God, who stoppeth the pain and stoppeth the blood," she muttered.

"This is bullshit," said Zee, grabbing her arm and trying to pull her away. She slipped, her palm skidding across a puddle of blood. Hurriedly she wiped her hand on her jeans.

Clarence slapped him on the arm and told him to hush. "You keep right on going, honey," he said to Bethany as she looked up at him. "Don't stop." He looked at the others. "If you've got any brains . . . pray!"

She nodded her head and closed her eyes once more, beginning the chant again, repeating the words in an unending litany, her hands outstretched. At first, their prayerful mutterings were disconcerting, but she allowed herself to fall into the energy. Her fingers tingled and the heat grew in her palms. Confidence spread through her as she felt the familiar peace and strength of the healing energy as it pulsed through her body. She grabbed onto that confidence, feeling the surge of power. Finally, as always when doing a healing, she saw the eyes of her guardian before her own—big, cat-wide eyes that signaled the healing was blessed and all was in the hands of Spirit. Still, she did not quit. Balanced on her haunches, she began to rock, losing the sense of time and place, thinking only of stopping the blood. *Release the worry, do the work,* echoed Ramona's voice in her mind.

"I'll be darned," whispered Zee. "The bleeding's stopped."

Bethany could hear the wail of the ambulance siren along the ridge.

Clarence helped her to her feet. Her legs cramped and her knees buckled, but Clarence kept her steady. "You're one of the girls I hired yesterday. What's your name again?"

"Bethany," she said quietly, looking at the injured Tad. He had the same facial structure as the girl with the golf cart she'd seen earlier, though her hair carried more fire. His eyes, she recalled from that first moment when she entered the shed, were that same mystical blue. This must definitely be one of the twins—the girl the other. "My name is Bethany Salem," she said.

Clarence grinned, his gray-white whiskers dancing along the folds of his wizened face. He took off his green and orange baseball cap. "Pleased to meet you, young Bethany. Who taught you how to pow-wow? I didn't think there was any more of them folks around."

Bethany looked at the three men, not quite sure what to say. *My Creole housekeeper taught me. You see, I'm a Witch.* Oh, no! That wouldn't do at all.

"What's Pow-Wow?" asked Zee, his heavy face showing an expression of doubt yet a hint of interest, as if he was filing the information away for later use.

"A system of faith healing," answered Clarence. "Used to be a lot of them in these parts, but with all the development over the years and all them fancy medical doctors, there aren't too many left. In fact, I thought they were all gone." He looked at Bethany. "But I guess I was wrong."

The ambulance squealed into the parking lot. The medical personnel rushed into the grading shed, followed by Nam.

"Where's that blasted ice?" shouted Old Man Bindart, looking around the shed. Alice stood by the conveyor belt, the ice dripping from her plump, shaking hands. She looked at Bethany, her slit-eyes filled with loathing. How long had Alice the Malice been standing there? There was at least a cup of water on the concrete floor. Alice handed the dripping bag to Zee.

"It was her fault Tad is hurt," said Alice, her voice ascending to a murderous falsetto as she pointed a wet, accusing finger at Bethany. "She came in here right before the accident. They were horsing around and she pushed Tad into the conveyor belt. I saw her do it!"

Bethany, not believing what she heard, opened her mouth to protest.

Nam rushed to Bethany's side. "That's a lie! Bethany wasn't even here! Tad was showing me how the conveyor belt works and it jammed. He stuck his hand in to fix it. No one was in here but the two of us. Clarence was out getting some more jugs for the cider machine. No one pushed anybody!"

Alice's lip curled. "She lies."

Old Man Bindart turned to Bethany, his shoulders shaking, the bill of his green hat emblazoned with "Tractor Pull USA Champion" bobbing up and down. "You're fired! You can take your friends with you. You're nothing but the devil's own!" he screamed, shaking a gnarled finger at Bethany and Nam. "How else would you have been able to stop that blood? You hurt him and then you tried to fix it. Just like a demon trying to work a false miracle. Alice told me earlier you all are evil Witches. Been in the paper! I don't care if your father is a cop! He can be the top cop for all I care! You can collect the black girl at the top of the ridge. Don't come back here, ever!"

Alice snickered spitefully. Nam's lower lip trembled, the rims of her eyes filling with tears as Bethany led her out the door. Bethany, on the other hand, felt the rage building within her, the explosive anger curdling her blood. All day she'd put up with abuse, and now this! When a shelf brimming with fruit cans crashed to the floor behind her, resulting in a high-pitched squeal from Alice, Bethany never bothered to turn her head.

Chapter 4

"I didn't see it coming," said Bethany, shoving her straw up and down in the lid of her soda. She felt grungy and filthy from the day's work but agreed to stop at the Taco Bell with the others before they went home. She washed up in the restaurant bathroom, staring at her reflection, worrying that others might stare at the blood on her jeans. She tried to wash it out with restaurant soap and a wad of paper towels, but she made an even bigger mess. A middle-aged lady with a kid looked at the bloody water and hustled the child out of the restroom without using it. Bethany stared at herself in the mirror. She even had dirt in her hair! Ugh. This whole day felt so surreal.

Nam and Tillie didn't look any better than she did. Most of the customers politely ignored them, a few stared, but no one said anything. "Alice the Malice is a real piece of work. I've got to hand it to her, that was quick thinking, blaming the accident on us," Bethany said, carrying the bright red tray laden with food to a corner booth.

Tillie bit into a taco, the salsa dribbling down her brown arm. "I don't even know the girl, and in one day she rips our new jobs right out from underneath us. I definitely do not like her." She wiped her arm with a napkin, the jingle of her bracelets lost in the racket of the restaurant.

"I told you again this morning that the place gave me a bad feeling," sniffed Nam as she twirled her green dangling earrings with flashing emerald-painted nails. "Ramona said we should pay attention to our gut feelings. I wish I had."

"It's my fault," said Bethany. "I pushed you both into it. I get sick of adults telling me what to do. I want to make my own decisions, and I want them to be right, but that isn't always the case."

"Don't beat yourself up over it," said Tillie. "We all needed the money."

Nam looked at Bethany. "You didn't make that shelf fall, did you? I mean, I've seen you do some strange stuff."

Bethany tossed her head. "What if I did? Serves them right."

"But that would be wrong," Nam replied fearfully. "I mean, we joke around a lot about having that kind of ability, and we've all experienced uncanny flukes, but if you can really do those things, you'd better be careful."

"Well, I can't," said Bethany, popping some food in her mouth and chewing noisily just to irritate Nam. "I'll 'fess up. It wasn't me. Maybe it was Janet's ghost—the one that walks in the butterfly garden, wherever that is! Who knows? That shelf was full of heavy cans. It was probably just over-loaded and gave way. No big deal." Bethany ignored Tillie's condescending gaze.

Nam didn't look especially convinced, either.

The Taco Bell buzzed with the chatter of adults, squealing children, and giggling teens. The noise was giving Bethany a headache. "I just can't believe any of it," she said dully. "I hope Tad is all right."

"Ask Nam," said Tillie. "She's the gossip mill of the universe."

"Just a minute," replied Nam, wiping her dainty mouth. Cell phone in hand, she made a quick call. "My cousin is a candystriper at the hospital," she informed them, head tilting, waiting for a response. "I called her on the way over here and asked her to keep an eye out for info." She raised her head, adjusting the phone slightly, sticking her finger in her other ear. "What's the news?" she asked into the cell phone. She nodded, quickly ended the call, and slapped the phone shut. "He's in recovery. They put his finger back on. It looks good, or so she says. Everyone's talking about the time written on his forehead in black marker. Some of the nurses want to meet the crazy girl with brains. That would be you," she directed at Bethany.

Tillie sulked. "Man, I'm out there working in that darned orchard and you two have all the fun and I've got blisters to prove it!" She held out her puffy palms, then began devouring a second taco.

"I wouldn't call a severed finger *fun*," remarked Nam.

"So much for your shake-and-bake job magick," muttered Tillie, glaring at Nam.

"Me!" the girl exclaimed. "Oh, blame it all on little Nam! I don't think so!"

"Yeah, Nam," said Bethany in a teasing voice. "Here I was, apologizing, beating myself up, and it was really all your fault."

Nam's eyes narrowed. "Didn't you say you were working magick for a job, too?"

Bethany smiled. "Sorry, just venting, I guess. That Alice girl was horrible!"

"You can say that again," replied Nam. "I can't believe she told such a whopper of a lie. Why would someone do something like that?"

Bethany's eyes drifted over the crowded restaurant as she contemplated Alice's behavior. "She could have put the tanglefoot beneath the steps but I looked at her aura, and I don't think she has it in her."

"What are you talking about?" asked Tillie. "What tanglefoot? Where did you find one of those?" She reached for her soda.

Bethany told the girls of her discovery of the charm before the accident.

"Wow," said Nam, shivering. "Who would want to curse the Bindarts?"

"What did you do with it?" asked Tillie, her dark eyes sparkling with interest.

"Nothing," answered Bethany. "I left it there. I was going to pick it up later, but then the accident happened."

Tillie's jaw dropped. "You *left* it there? If we don't go get it and take care of it, that magick will keep right on working. The accident this morning was bad enough. Who knows what else could happen."

"I think it's been there awhile," said Bethany, "protected from the weather because it was so deep under the porch. The accident was probably just that—an accident, nothing more. Tad took one look at Nam's girlish figure in that jungle-green outfit and lost all sense of reality."

Nam made a mean pixie face. "Very funny."

"You are adorable," said Bethany sweetly, her face stretched to keep from laughing. "So what was he like—Tad, I mean?"

Nam's face took on a dreamy quality. "Muscles, sunburn, an excellent sense of humor."

"So what you are telling me," said Tillie, "is that a home-schooled boy has the same basic equipment as anyone else."

Nam stuck out her tongue. "He writes poetry. In fact, he was reciting some when the accident happened."

Bethany groaned.

Tillie closed her eyes then slowly opened them. "You mean he was putting the make on you when he got his finger chopped off."

Nam picked at her taco. "You could say that."

Bethany slapped her palm to her forehead while Tillie burst out laughing. "I've heard of people losing their heads for love, but never a finger."

"That's not funny!" exclaimed Nam, her eyes widened in horror. "It was a serious injury!"

Bethany soothed her feelings by saying, "Of course it was serious."

Tillie rolled her eyes.

In an obvious effort to change the subject, Nam said, "I find it hard to believe that a little ball of wire could cause such a fuss. Besides, remember Ramona told us that something like that doesn't work very well. You've got to put a lot of effort into it and then, if you succeed, you have to worry about the negative energy coming back on you. What you wish for others is always what you eventually receive. Why would someone be so dumb as to make one in the first place?" She flicked a piece of lettuce across the table with her long, green nails.

"I wonder what other things have been happening at that orchard?" remarked Tillie, half to herself. "Janet mentioned strange things. Something about a fire. Maybe we should call her?"

Bethany shook her head. "Alice the Malice told me that Janet visited her last night. They must be friends. Janet is also the one that told Alice that we were Wiccan, along with a ton of rumors." She looked pointedly at Nam, who looked away uncomfortably.

"That Janet jerk set us up!" growled Tillie. The colorful beads in her hair quivered as she moved her neck back and forth, a cool Cleopatra action that only Tillie could get away with.

"Janet didn't cause the accident unless she's somehow invisible," spat Nam. "But, okay, we've seen some pretty unusual things . . . maybe it was the tanglefoot."

Bethany said, "No, you were probably right the first time. That thing is just a simple folk charm meant to scare more than anything else. Didn't Ramona tell us that those kinds of magicks don't work unless the recipient believes in them?"

Nam continued to contemplate her taco. "Yeah. Besides, we can't go back. Bindart told us we weren't allowed on the property. Let him deal with it." Her green eyes flashed with indignation. "He was really mean to us. And I sure don't want to mess with any ghosts, either," she said flatly, looking directly at Bethany. "I've had enough of that woo-woo stuff. Give me good old mathematical astrology any day and I'll be delighted."

"There you go with that ghost thing again," said Tillie. "Forget what Janet said. She probably thought Alice was the walking horror, and rightfully so. Sounds to me like Janet is two-faced."

Bethany laughed. "You've got that right, but Alice the Malice isn't much better! In a way, I feel sorry for her. Remember how Gillian used to act?"

There were knowing head-nods all around.

"You know," said Tillie. "No one knows where Janet lives, and she won't ever let anyone drive her home after debate club. Once, when her father didn't come to pick her up, she took a taxi home."

"That's weird," said Bethany.

"She has a boyfriend," volunteered Nam.

Tillie raised an eyebrow. "How do you know that?"

"She told me."

Tillie shook her head. "I think Janet speaks with forked tongue. I bet she doesn't really have a boyfriend at all. She probably just made one up."

Nam indicated the opposite. "No, he picked her up from school once. I saw the car, but I couldn't see him very well."

Her curiosity piqued, Bethany asked, "What kind of car was it?"

"Dunno. I wasn't really paying attention. All I can remember is Janet saying that her boyfriend was there, and off she went. I only remember because it was at lunch time, and Janet was going home early. I just assumed that her boyfriend was an older guy because it was in the middle of the day, and obviously he wasn't in school. After all, she is a senior, and lots of them date boys in college or guys out of school."

Bethany surveyed her friends. "Have you ever noticed anything funny about her?"

"Like what?" asked Tillie. "To me, she's just a jerk."

"What do you mean?" asked Nam.

"I don't know. Like something creepy," remarked Bethany.

"That kohl eye makeup doesn't help," replied Tillie. "That's a new twist since September. She didn't wear that stuff when we started school this year."

"You've been watching too many horror shows," said Nam.

"Amen to that, girl!" said Tillie, slapping the table. "Last weekend you stayed up all night watching horror flicks. I, on the other hand, had the sense to get some sleep. You're mixing real life with Hollywood."

Nam dipped her head. "Especially since real life has been a bit," she seemed to grope for the right word, "*unusual* for us these past three months. Most people wouldn't believe the stuff we've seen."

"You said you checked out Alice's aura," said Tillie, wiggling her fingers. "Did you look at Janet?"

"Didn't think of it," said Bethany. "Never had any reason to. Most of the time I forget I can do it. I have to admit that I've been floating around in my own little mental world, and besides, I really don't want to know about all the crap people drag around with them. It's depressing. Besides, I'm not even sure I'm doing it right. If she was into anything strange, we would have known about it by now, wouldn't we?"

No one answered.

Finally, Nam giggled. "It's not depression, you just miss Sidney."

"That'll do it," said Tillie. "She's lovesick."

Bethany playfully slapped Tillie on the arm. "Am not."

"Maybe you should check her out at school on Monday," said Tillie.

"Won't do us any good now," said Bethany. "We lost the jobs."

Tillie made a gurgling noise with her straw. "Too bad. There goes the free fruit. Did you see some of those apples? I've never seen such big ones . . . and red!"

"Poison apples, more like it," sniffed Nam. "Eat them all your life and you get mean, like Old Man Bindart, who probably keeps his kids locked up in the attic!"

"Not with Tad's suntan," reminded Bethany.

Tillie threw her wadded napkin at Nam. "You've got a way too vivid imagination, girl! Hey! Speaking of conjuring things in your mind, isn't that Janet Atkins sitting over there with your favorite nemesis, René Farmore?"

"You're joking!" whispered Bethany. "I don't want to turn around. It'll look like I care. What's she doing?"

Nam winced. "They're laughing at us and pointing at our table."

Bethany could feel her temper building.

"If Janet has a boyfriend, you sure wouldn't know it," remarked Tillie. "Look how she's sucking up to that guy sitting at the next table."

"Maybe that's her boyfriend," offered Nam.

Tillie shook her head. "Not if he's sitting at a different table."

"I'm not going to lower my dignity and turn around," stated Bethany.

"Another guy just sat down." Her slim fingers danced across the table. "With the first guy, not with the girls. Both guys look like rednecks. They have jean jackets and denim pants. A little like Tad, but not as cute," said Nam as if she was announcing a fashion show on the radio. "René is wearing Mudd jeans and a really cool shirt with red piping. Janet has on some dark Goth stuff. Some sort of black netting on the sleeves. Probably bought it at that new store in the mall. I'll have you know that store is wicked expensive. Her shoes don't match. They're all scuffed and beaten. And she's got that kohl makeup on again. I wonder what's gotten into her. René, though . . . Wait. René just got up and headed toward the bathroom. Janet is alone. The guys are turning around, ignoring Janet. Obviously the main attraction has just left the stage. Switch places with me and you can check out her aura."

"Won't that look a bit obvious?" asked Bethany.

"Who cares," said Tillie. "Just do it."

"But I'm not that good at it," whined Bethany.

Nam got up and literally slid into Bethany's seat. She either had to endure the spectacle of Nam sitting on her lap or move quickly. She chose to move. Bethany settled in beside Tillie and looked at Janet, trying not to be obvious. Janet, no longer the center of attention, stared uncomfortably at the soda in front of her, not paying attention to anyone in the restaurant. Bethany de-focused, allowing her eyes to relax. It took more than one try, but finally she could see a thin film around Janet's head. Not a brighter place, like usual, but a dim ghostly gray. Now and then something black popped through it, then quickly receded. Something almost like . . . Bethany searched her mind for an association . . . like a black snake. No . . . worm. She shivered.

"What?" asked Nam. "What are you seeing?"

Tillie cocked her head. "Whatever it is, it isn't pretty. I can tell by the expression on Bethany's face."

"It's gross," said Bethany. "Like a gray fog with black worms in it."

"Eeuuw!" squealed Nam. "Yuck!"

"Hey!" Tillie whispered. "René's back. What's her aura look like?"

"Puke green," replied Bethany. "With yellow speckles."

Nam leaned forward. "What does that mean?"

"Beats me," said Bethany. "I just see 'em, I've no clue how to read 'em."

"Hold on to your hats, ladies. Janet has finally seen us. She's coming over."

Nam rubbed her forehead. "Oh, dear," she muttered. "This isn't going to be pretty."

Tillie spoke first, striking the opening volley. "So what's with the Goth?"

Janet's kohl eyes narrowed. "So what's with all that plastic in your hair? And I bet that's not even your hair. I bet it's some dead horse's tail."

Tillie started to rise, but Bethany held her down. "Don't mind Tillie," Bethany said. "We were just wondering why all the dark makeup and Dracula clothes. I mean, it's different, that's all."

Janet passed over the clothing discussion and went right for the gusto. "Heard you were fired today. That you managed to mutilate Tad Bindart. Nice going. I always knew the three of you were bloodsuckers."

"That's it," said Tillie. "I wanna deck her."

Janet scoffed. "You and who's army? These two pathetic creatures?" she asked glancing at Nam and Bethany.

Nam spoke up. "I take offense to that. I may not be an army, but I'm certainly not pathetic."

"No, that's right, Nam. You're not pathetic, you just throw yourself at any guy wearing pants. There's a word for that, you know."

Nam blinked several times. "What are you talking about?"

Janet put her hand on her hip and laughed. "Isn't that how you got into trouble last month? Stealing someone else's guy?"

Nam's normally pale face colored.

Tillie stood up. "That's it. She's toast."

Bethany rose quickly, making sure she was between Tillie and Janet. "I think you should just leave, Janet," said Bethany quietly. "You set us up at the orchard. You knew that once Mr. Bindart found out we were Witches, he'd fire us. From what I can see, you wanted to humiliate us. I don't understand why. We've never done anything to you. You've had your fun. Buzz off."

Janet didn't move. "I had my reasons," she said.

Tillie tried to push past Bethany, but Bethany held her arm. "She isn't worth it."

By now people at the tables around them were staring. René Farmore walked over with the two guys in tow. "Causing a scene again, Bethany? Don't mind her, Janet. She doesn't get enough attention so she creates it. What are you talking to these peons for, anyway?"

Janet laughed and turned away.

"Her ancestors must be very angry," remarked Nam.

Bethany watched as Janet, René, and the boys exited the restaurant, laughing loudly. "Why?"

"Because they have sent the worms to eat her mind."

Tillie looked at her watch. "I've got to go. I'm supposed to be at cheerleading practice." She looked pointedly at Bethany. "We want to look good for the competition next week. Football may be over, but our coach thought we did such a good job during the fall season that she's entered us in some championship. We're working on a new routine."

"Uh, yeah," replied Bethany, picking up the cue. "I promised Ramona I'd try to be home before dark. Besides, I have a test to study for."

Nam pulled out of the parking lot first, waving goodbye as she sped through the parked cars.

"Girl better learn to slow down," said Tillie, shivering in the frigid air as they watched Nam's taillights merge with the highway traffic. "Are you thinking what I'm thinking?"

"Oh! Don't go there!" said Bethany, holding up a gloved hand.

"What time do they close the orchard store?" asked Tillie, hurrying to her dented and rusted Toyota squatting at the edge of the Taco Bell parking lot.

"This is a bad idea, Tillie."

"What time?"

Bethany groaned. "Seven, but the grading shed stays open till past nine."

"Maybe not since there was an accident today," remarked Tillie as she opened her car door. The hinges squealed.

Bethany shook her head. "This is the end of the season. I know that much from Alice the Malice. They'll work no matter what." She dug in her black raincoat pocket for her keys, shivering in the stiff breeze of the autumn dusk. "Boy, do I miss summer," she mumbled. "I'm either going to have to find a liner for this coat or dig out my winter jacket from last year. I can't afford a new one."

"You could ask your dad," suggested Tillie.

"Oh, like you ask yours?"

"I see your point." Tillie leaned on her car door. "Then I'll meet you at your house around nine. I'll tell my parents I'm sleeping over. We can get that tanglefoot then. I'd come with you now but I don't want to miss practice. We'll just go in and get out. Slick. Easy. No one will know, and we've done our good deed for the day."

Bethany frowned. "I don't know, Tillie. Maybe Nam's right. Maybe we should just leave it. Write this whole mess off as a bad experience and spend our time looking for another job. I hear there's a book superstore opening where Bowman's used to be. Maybe we three could get in there."

"Listen," said Tillie, her warm breath fanning white mist in the cold air. "We took an oath of dedication saying that we'd work for the good of all. We can't let that thing stay there. We know what it is. We know how to take it apart."

"We do?"

"Don't we? Well, even if we don't, we can figure it out. Who knows what else might happen if we just let it go? We could ask Ramona."

Bethany squinted her eyelids. "Like Ramona would really approve of that. She'll tell us that we should be studying rather than doing, or that it's none of our business—and she'd be right about that," said Bethany, hearing the excuse for what it was—hollow and lame. Tillie just stared at her, those dark eyes boring into her brain. Finally Bethany threw up her gloved hands and relented. "Okay, okay. You win. Meet me at nine tonight. I still think this is a bad idea," she said, unlocking her car door, but Tillie didn't hear her. She'd already hopped in her car and rumbled out of the parking lot, trailing black smoke and leaving the stench of oil in her wake.

"And when we get it, what are we going to do with it?" mumbled Bethany sourly as she shoved the key in the ignition. As if she didn't have enough regular homework, now she had more research to do, and it wasn't as easy as getting out a dictionary or encyclopedia. She'd have to start digging in Ramona's library—not an easy task without explaining what she was looking for.

"I can't believe how cold it is," said Bethany, trying to draw the collar of her black raincoat closer to her throat.

"Quit whining," said Tillie, huffing behind her. They'd parked Bethany's red Camaro off Old Mill Road a few feet into the orchard.

"What if someone sees us?" asked Bethany, giggling despite her paranoia.

"What are you laughing at?" growled Tillie. "If anyone asks, we'll just tell them we're out spotting deer. It's a fairly popular hobby in this area. Come on, the store's past this line of fruit trees. We're coming in from the back, so we'll be passing the house where the migrant workers stay. I went this way this afternoon." Their feet crunched on the frosty ground.

"How do you know who is in that house?" asked Bethany, jamming her hands deep in her pockets. Her fingers wrapped around the cold barrel of the flashlight at the bottom. She shivered. The other pocket held a mini cell phone, and the bill was due on that baby, too. She mentally groaned.

"The guy I was working with this morning told me. He's staying there along with his brother and some other guys. There's some ladies, too, but Old Man Bindart has them in a cheap hotel a mile or so down the road. Bindart's funny about mixing the sexes. Even the work crews are either all male, or all female. You all pick in the same area, but you're supposed to stick with your crew and not wander off. They even do a head count several times a day."

"That's odd," said Bethany. "Rules like that mean something has happened in the past and the management is trying to make sure it doesn't happen again."

"Or it means Old Man Bindart is just plain weird. Take your pick."

Bethany tripped over an exposed root and almost bit the ground with her teeth. She could hear loud music coming from the rambling migrant house. She hoped it was too cold for anyone to be loitering outside because she didn't relish the thought of crawling on the cold ground past the place. "I can't believe you talked me into this," she complained.

"Shh!" commanded Tillie, putting a finger to her lips. "We're too close to the house. Someone might hear you."

The ivory siding of the domicile glowed eerily against the dark, star-speckled sky. Their accelerated breath fogged the snapping air under their noses. Not a soul seemed to be outside, but the wild noise squeezing out onto the lawn meant that some sort of party was in progress. It was, after all, Saturday night and the long hours of orchard work demanded, Bethany supposed, equally hard hours of concentrated relaxation. There were several vehicles parked in the yard, including a few trucks with gun racks, a battered compact car that looked worse than Tillie's Toyota, and a vintage Buick with air-brushed flames racing along the sides. Bethany rolled her eyes. This was definitely not a good idea. Anything could happen to them out here.

The moon was up and the lemon-yellow light spilling from the windows allowed them to see enough to creep past the big house without incident, then scurry through a deadened garden plot and around the back of the Bindart store. A lone security light on a driveway post gleamed weakly. It was enough so that Bethany could tell the tanglefoot when she found it. Since there were no windows in the grading shed across the driveway, there was no way to know if anyone remained on this area of the property. At least there weren't any cars. One dim light illuminated the interior of the store, but little of it seeped into the darkness. Every now and then a loud guffaw from the white house blatted through the night.

"Do you think this place is really haunted?" asked Tillie, crouching by the front porch of the country store.

"Now's a great time to bring that up," grumbled Bethany, busily searching for the tanglefoot. She was afraid to use the flashlight for fear someone would spot them. She didn't really want to use her bare hands and cursed herself for not remembering to bring along gloves. She'd had them back at the Taco Bell. Drat! Probably sitting on the console of her car where she left them. Delicately her fingers traced the ground around the bottom step. All she could feel were a few dead leaves and something ooey-gooey. Where was the darned thing?

Tillie edged over beside her. "Did you find it yet?"

"No."

"Get it and let's get out of here," said Tillie testily.

"I can't feel it!" complained Bethany.

Tillie stiffened. "Did you hear that?" she whispered.

Irritated, Bethany turned around. "Hear what?"

"That moaning sound."

Bethany shook her head. "It's probably your stomach." She turned back, continuing to grope in the dark under the steps.

Tillie grabbed the back of Bethany's coat. "There! I heard it again!" Her voice carried a hint of amusement.

"For heaven's sake," spat Bethany, "will you get a grip? You're the one that wanted to come out here. Stop making things up just to scare me!" Bethany's cold fingers touched pointy metal, but Tillie bumped her and the object skittered further under the step. She hoped that Zee fellow wasn't around. She sure wouldn't want to meet him out here in the dark. Bethany turned around to shake some sense into Tillie, except Tillie was gone.

The eerie notes of a fiddle swept through the parking lot, then died softly in the night as Bethany's heart waltzed into possible failure.

Chapter 5

Shoulders shaking, Bethany stared into the business end of a shotgun, moonlight glinting off cold steel.

"Who are you and what are you doing here?" demanded a female voice.

Bethany desperately looked for Tillie, but couldn't locate her in the cavernous shadows of Bindart's Orchard. As she hadn't heard a shot, and Tillie wasn't slumped at Bethany's feet, it was safe to assume Tillie spirited herself into the darkness.

"I'll count to three," said the woman ruthlessly. "If you don't speak up, I'll shoot."

"Bethany!" she exclaimed. "My name is Bethany Salem."

The gun didn't move. Not even a tremor. "What are you doing here?"

Bethany could feel her eyes roving. *Be calm. Be normal.* What had Ramona taught them about glamories? *Think it, be it. Think it, be it.* She concentrated on being nonthreatening. Angelic. "I worked here today and I . . . I dropped my lipstick out of my purse in my hurry to leave, and I thought I might find it here, so I came looking for it." The deer-spotting story was out. There was no way she could claim that she was looking for a deer under the steps of the Bindart Orchard store.

"Why didn't you just wait until morning?"

Bethany dug her hands deep in her pockets, glad that the darkness hid the dirt and grime from digging around under the steps. "I just bought it in New York City. I paid over twenty dollars . . . and . . . and I was told I wasn't allowed to come back here."

"Why is that?"

Bethany shifted uncomfortably. "Someone claimed I did something that I really didn't. It's a long story."

The gun remained pointed at her chest. "Where's your car?"

Uh-oh, thought Bethany. *How do I explain that my car is parked half a mile away?* "I walked," she fibbed, well . . . it really wasn't a lie. She had walked up the road from the car.

"From where?"

"Listen, it's really cold out here. Can I just go?" asked Bethany, trying to keep a whine out of her voice. *Think it, be it.*

"Bethany Salem," repeated the woman slowly. "You're that girl. The one that stopped the blood and all. Is that right?"

Oh, boy, thought Bethany. *Now the gun goes off.* Finally Bethany nodded. She hoped the woman hadn't believed Alice's story or she just might shoot Bethany if she thought the accident was her fault. Bethany tensed, but the woman lowered the gun. Bethany's breath came out in a whoosh, spraying the night air with heated moisture.

"My grandfather could do that. Stop blood. You sure amazed Zee. My name's Leslee Bindart," said the woman, slinging the gun over her shoulder and holding out her hand.

Bethany shook the cold fingers, feeling the calluses on the woman's palm. Leslee Bindart wore an old camouflage coat and a battered baseball cap with the bill at the back of her head. What was it with these people and baseball caps? A farmer fashion statement? The way the woman stood smacked of ex-military.

"You in the armed services at one time?" asked Bethany.

The woman stiffened. "It shows? Marines. I talked to Clarence this afternoon. He says you really helped the boy. Thank you. I'm sorry you lost something in your rush to leave."

Bethany gave her a wavering smile. "It's okay."

"Did you find it?"

"What?"

"The lipstick."

You dork, Bethany chided herself. She quickly shook her head.

"Maybe you can see it at daylight," said Leslee.

"Ah. Mr. Bindart told us not to come back. That's why I came this evening." Which wasn't a lie.

Leslee waved her hand in the air. "Oh, him. He felt bad once he got the story straight. When Tad regained consciousness after the surgery, he explained everything to our father. The Asian girl was right. Tad did it to himself. If you still want a job, you and your friends can come back. Just keep out of my father's way. He's not been the most pleasant person lately. Stress. Deal with either me or Clarence. We're short on help right now, and the pickings are slim."

"That would be great!" said Bethany, although she wasn't so sure if she ever wanted to come back here. Screw the tanglefoot and screw these crazy people. Where was Tillie, anyway?

"Can I give you a ride home?"

Bethany's head snapped up. "No, thank you. I'll be fine," she said. "I'll talk to my friends about the jobs. By the way, do you play the fiddle?"

Leslee Bindart looked at her strangely. "No. Why? Who have you been talking to?" she asked, a hint of suspicion lacing her voice.

"Just wondered," said Bethany, trying to sound as upbeat as possible. "I guess the guys in the white house over there were playing CDs."

"Maybe," answered Leslee. "They can get loud. Now you get on home. You know, you shouldn't slink around. People might get the wrong idea. And I'd lose that black raincoat."

"Uh. Right," answered Bethany, backing away quickly. From the corner of her eye she thought she saw a white face peering out at her from the windows of the orchard store, but when she turned slightly to get a better look, no one was there. Bethany hurried down the Bindart driveway, aware of Leslee's eyes boring into her retreating back. At least she assumed it was Leslee.

Tillie caught up with her halfway down the road. "Where were you?" asked Bethany, grabbing Tillie's arm and shaking her.

"Hey, I figured that if she caught just one of us, the other could get help if necessary. I hid around the side of the store. I couldn't believe that she offered to give our jobs back!"

Bethany shivered. "I hated lying to her."

"Oh, and you were going to tell her that you were after a cursed bit of wire? That would have gone over really well. Did you find the tanglefoot?" asked Tillie, stepping up the pace as they hurried down Old Mill Road.

"No. I almost had it. At least I think I did." The heels of their boots clattered on the macadam. "I don't think the car is too much further," puffed Bethany. "Did you see anyone in the store?"

Tillie shook her head. "No, there wasn't much light. I could hardly see the two of you."

A blast of headlights topped the hill and roared toward them. The girls edged along the side of the road, thinking the vehicle would simply pass them.

There was plenty of room. The engine growled and the mass of metal surged forward, aiming directly at the girls, capturing their shocked forms in the laser-sharp blaze of its headlights.

"Move!" screamed Tillie, grabbing Bethany's arm and pulling her into the orchard. They hit a ditch and rolled down the embankment, the speeding vehicle swerving at the last moment, red taillights gleaming like receding devil eyes in the darkness.

"That was close," huffed Tillie, pulling Bethany to her feet. "Are you okay?"

Bethany couldn't stop shaking. There was no way whoever was driving that car could not have seen them. Even if the driver didn't see Bethany because of the black coat, surely they would have seen Tillie's champagne jacket. It was as if the person behind that wheel purposefully tried to kill them! "I banged up my leg," said Bethany, "but other than that, I think I'm all right."

"Too weird," said Tillie, brushing off her coat. "Must have been a drunk. Man, would you look at this? Even in the dark I can see the stains on my coat. How am I going to explain this to my mother? I'll have to get it cleaned before she sees it. She lent me the money for it. If I were you, I'd ditch that black coat."

A rustling, cracking sound split the night and both girls whirled toward the darkness of the orchard. Three deer—two doe and a buck—burst from between the trees and leapt up the embankment, over the ditch, and clattered across the road.

Bethany's heart thudded in her chest.

"I have to pee," said Tillie, her voice quavering in the darkness. "I mean I *really* have to pee!"

Ramona sat in the plush cushion rocker in the family room before a toasty fire. A mystery novel lay abandoned on the arm of the chair. Now and then Ramona tossed a few herbs into the flames from a red enamel bowl in her lap, mumbling in French. Tillie and Bethany watched the cavorting spirals of fire, ash, and smoke, saying nothing, breathing in the pleasant, spicy perfume of the herbal concoction. Bethany rubbed her aching leg, her thoughts cavorting over the evening's events. Hecate perched on the sofa, a green felt catnip mouse firmly taloned between his paws.

Bethany, sprawled out on the floor with a pillow, roused herself long enough to ask Ramona what she thought she was doing.

"Ramona is looking for the truth," said the housekeeper, relaxing back into the chair.

"The truth about what?" asked Bethany suspiciously. Part of her wanted to share the information about the tanglefoot and this evening's adventure, but another part wanted to keep the excitement to herself, to savor her experiences only with her friends, but Ramona had pried most of it out of them.

"There are all sorts of truth," said Ramona.

Bethany hated it when the housekeeper tried to be wise. It was annoying.

"And how are you going to discover the truth?" asked Tillie, her tone indicating she was oblivious to Ramona's soothsaying abilities, or at least was too lazy to think about it right now.

"By reading the flames," said Ramona.

"Couldn't we just pop popcorn?" asked Tillie, the beads in her hair clicking softly as she turned her head. The grandfather clock in the hall ticked like a human heartbeat.

Ramona didn't answer.

Bethany reached over and picked up the bowl of herbs, sniffing the contents. The herbs didn't smell bad, but they made her nose tickle. "What's in here?" she asked, wrinkling her nose. Her own curiosity aroused that of the cat. As soon as she set the bowl down, he slithered over to investigate, took one hefty snort, then sneezed repeatedly. He glared at Bethany as if she should have warned him.

Staring steadily at the fire, Ramona answered, "A bit of broom, some ground orange peel, orris root, the dried head of a dandelion, and crushed ivy. Oh, and pumpkin spice."

"Like in a pie?" asked Tillie, licking her lips.

Hecate strolled over to Tillie, then pounced on her stomach, batting at the beads in her hair. She squealed.

Ramona smiled. "Food. All pretty Tillie ever thinks of is food!"

Bethany laid back and adjusted the pillow beneath her head, gazing at the fire. A pine log popped and sputtered. "I don't see a darned thing in those flames," she said irritably.

"Me neither," replied Tillie. "Looks orange, red, and yellow to me. I don't think we should work at Bindart's. I think we should look for a job someplace else. Even if we go back there tomorrow, they'll still treat us like we're weird, and I don't know about you but I'm sick and tired of people thinking we're bad news because we're different."

Bethany rolled over on her stomach and looked at Tillie. "We need the money."

Ramona rocked methodically, eyes now partially closed. Earlier, when the girls tried to sneak in the door, Ramona stood on the stoop, a formidable, entrenched barrier with broom in hand, demanding to know what they'd been up to. There was no recourse but to tell her—most of it. Now, Ramona appeared to contemplate Bethany's comments, or so Bethany assumed.

Finally, Ramona said, "Bethany, you left the part out about the fiddle."

Bethany, slightly dozy, sat upright, blinking. "What's that got to do with it?"

Ramona threw more herbs on the fire, watched the flames closely, then said, "A great deal, if my ancestors are correct. And, *cherie*, they have never been wrong. What is the *jardin papillion*?"

"Huh?"

"The butterfly garden?"

"You're creeping me out, Ramona. I don't know. A garden there, I guess. Some girl at school tried to tell us it was haunted."

"What girl?" asked Ramona with a suspicious expression.

"I didn't hear any fiddle," said Tillie, deftly ignoring any mention of Janet and looking from the bowl of herbs to the fire, a new respect for Ramona clearly showing in her eyes. "Your ancestors talk to you?"

"When necessary," said Ramona, slowly rising from the rocker.

"Can you teach me how to do that?"

Ramona smiled. "When you are ready. It takes time to learn to listen, but I think now we must concentrate on the matters at hand. Tillie? Ramona thinks you are correct. Returning to Bindart's would be a mistake. There is something odd and evil there. I am sure of it, but I am not confident the tanglefoot you found was recently placed under those stairs. Perhaps it was hidden there several months ago. It is evil, but I am not so sure it is a curse, exactly. Over the centuries, the tanglefoot has been used for many purposes, and not all of them precisely evil. I hope if someone finds it they have sense enough to throw it away. *Oui.* Yes. Better that you two leave snoozing alligators alone."

Bethany looked at Tillie with an I-told-you-so expression. She thought of her upcoming car payment and groaned. If she didn't make some money soon, she'd have to ask her dad for a loan and she definitely didn't want to do that! The speeches, the condescending attitude . . . she loved her father, but she could do without another lecture on personal finances.

"Ramona is going up to her room now," the housekeeper informed them. "Tillie? You did call your parents? They know you're here?"

Tillie nodded, stroking Hecate's ebony-black fur. "I'm hungry," said Tillie after Ramona retrieved her mystery novel and left the room. "Let's make some pizza!" She jumped up, practically throwing the cat in the air. Hecate hissed and landed daintily. "Oh, sorry, Hecate." The cat ignored her apology, bounding out of the family room.

Bethany covered her head with the pillow. "Having you for a friend is a guaranteed extra ten pounds on my hips," she muffled.

"Hey! I thought Ramona stayed in the apartment over the garage?" asked Tillie, dragging the pillow out of Bethany's clutches, then tossing it back to her.

"She still does," replied Bethany, getting to her feet, "but since we've gotten into so much trouble these last few months, my father insisted that she stay in a room upstairs when he's out of town. He fixed up the guest room for her last weekend."

"Bummer," said Tillie. "Now Ramona and her ancestors will see everything you do."

Bethany tilted her head and smiled. "It doesn't matter. With Ramona's radar, she seems to know anyway, but I've still got a trick or two up my sleeve. Some things should be sacred!"

Tillie snorted. "So where were your fancy tricks when we came home this evening? Ramona was planted on the doorstep like a giant Venus flytrap."

"Okay, so I'm not perfect," Bethany retorted. "If you don't shut up, I won't make that pizza."

"A cop's daughter into blackmail?" asked Tillie, a large grin on her face.

Bethany hit her with the pillow. "You know," she said, "I feel like I'm on the outside of this Bindart thing, looking in. Like there's obvious information that we're missing, and when we finally figure it out we'll have realized we were suffering from a blonde moment."

"Speak for yourself," said Tillie. "I ain't no blonde."

"It's not my logic, but my feelings. As if I'm floating around on the edges of something gruesome, trying like heck not to get sucked in."

Chapter 6

Sunday morning

From the attic window of the Bindart farmhouse, Cricket Bindart watched the November sun rise over South Mountain, the mountain itself a dark, violet smudge on the horizon. She sighed. Tad once told her about an article he'd read in a scientific journal that claimed sighing was a sign of stress. Well, maybe it was. The thought of Tad and his injury certainly didn't make her feel good. They were keeping him in the hospital. She'd wanted to go with him yesterday but her father would not permit it. With all the excitement, she'd almost forgotten about the dead rabbit and the note. Her stomach churned as she shivered and drew her white flannel nightgown around her.

She opened and closed her hands, trying to work the soreness out of her fingers. The same finger Tad injured especially hurt. Tad would say it was because they were twins and that they shared things beyond other peoples' understanding. Except they hardly shared anything anymore—other than pain. Tad was the brain of the family. Always reading. Always striving to learn more. Something was lost and she feared that the warm connection they once shared had fled their lives forever. It all started last summer when their father wouldn't allow Tad to get a computer—instead they'd both received the "outside world" speech. She and Tad always laughed about their father's odd fear of strangers, but Tad wasn't laughing anymore.

And neither was she.

A raven spun through the sky, screeching, calling. *To what?* she wondered. *To me?* When she saw those Witch girls at the orchard yesterday she couldn't believe her good fortune! They looked just like their pictures in the paper. Thanks to Alice, her only opening for help from them snapped shut like one of her dad's rusty old traps out in the barn. Then, later, her hopes soared. She'd been in the store last night when Bethany and Tillie were prowling around by the outside steps, watching them from the darkened store window. She was just about to go out and talk to them when Leslee appeared. What had they been doing by the steps of the store? What were they looking for? Would they come back?

She sat on the edge of her bed. If she were those girls, she wouldn't come back here to work, no matter what Leslee offered. How Cricket hated Alice! Stupid, meddling girl.

Okay. So they most likely won't come here, but that doesn't mean I can't go to them. They would have filled out forms yesterday before they started working. She'd sneak into the store, find the forms, and look up that Witch girl's address. While she was at it, she'd check under those front steps.

Quickly she flung open the sagging doors of the ancient chipped and scarred wardrobe, wondering for the millionth time what it would be like to live in a house that actually had closets.

Ramona bustled around the kitchen, her white billowy skirt dancing around her brown ankles. Bethany and Tillie stumbled into the kitchen, their faces puffy and belligerent.

"Why did you wake us up at seven on a Sunday morning?" complained Bethany, plopping down at the kitchen table. "If we aren't going to the orchard, we could've slept in." She leaned back in the chair and closed her eyes, her head nodding against her chest.

"Rise and shine!" shouted Ramona, clanging a pan with a wooden spoon.

Tillie moaned and sat opposite Bethany, cradling her head on the table, her beaded hair fanning across the red tablecloth like an exotic fan. "I told you we shouldn't have watched that last movie," she muttered. "But no! You had to see Alfred Hitchcock's *The Birds*!" She slowly lifted her head. "Is that bacon I smell? Sausage gravy? Home fries?" Her dark, glittering eyes honed in on the stove, her nose delicately sniffing the mouth-watering smells escaping from the pot lids. "Ooh, baby!"

she said, rubbing her hands together. "A real country breakfast morning! Ouch! Will you look at these blisters? I am not going back to that orchard ever again!"

"Food," muttered Bethany, squeezing her eyes shut again. "Yuck."

Ramona shook Bethany's shoulder roughly as she set down a steaming platter piled with sausage and potatoes. "Wake up, *ma cherie*! You are going to have company this morning. You need to be awake! Running a brush through that long hair of yours wouldn't be a bad idea, either. Right now you look like you stuck your finger in a light socket."

"That's my truly electric personality." Bethany popped one eye open, then closed it. "Tell whoever is coming to go away," she mumbled.

"No," said Ramona. "You will have to do that. It will be far better for all of us if you turn this person away, but I cannot make the decision for you. There is something very wrong with the Bindart family and things are about to get complicated. Ramona thinks you should be careful and not jump too hastily. You need to pay attention to your school studies and get a steady job that can meet your car payments. It is nice to help people, but sometimes such help can be expensive. You may not wish to pay the price." She held up her hand. "I will say no more, but I want you to be awake and thinking clearly, with a hot meal in your stomach!"

Bethany's curiosity was aroused. "Your ancestors talking to you again?"

Ramona shook her head. "No. A raven."

Bethany crossed her arms over her chest and closed her eyes again. "Yeah. Right. A bird. First Hitchcock, now you." As far as Bethany was concerned, Ramona was just a bit this side of crazy. Rabbits and ravens, it was becoming a regular wild kingdom around here.

"Please!" begged Cricket.

"I'm sorry, but we can't help you," replied Bethany.

The African-American girl stood in the background, peering over Bethany's shoulder as Bethany's hand firmly gripped the brass knob of the massive Wedgwood-blue front door.

Cricket's lower lip trembled. She'd sworn that she wasn't going to cry no matter what, but here she stood, pouring her heart out to two girls she'd never met properly and, worst of all, they were refusing to hear her out. They wouldn't even let her through the front door! She shivered uncontrollably, not knowing whether the reaction was from the frost-ridden November morning or internal despair.

The African-American girl—Tillie, wasn't it?— kept looking back into the depths of the house, as if she feared someone lurking there might overhear their conversation. What kind of strange people were these girls? Maybe her father was right. Maybe people outside her own environment weren't to be trusted after all. She made one last-ditch effort; the worst they could do was laugh at her. She tried one more time. "Please!"

Bethany stared at her with a stony expression.

Cricket swallowed dryly and turned to go, but Tillie reached forward and grabbed the edge of her coat, roughly jerking her back.

"Meet us at Cedar Crest Cemetery at noon," whispered Tillie. The front door closed with a re-sounding thud.

Cricket stood staring at the blue wooden door, her mouth hanging open. Should she go to the cemetery at noon, or should she just return home and stay there? Was this Tillie girl trying to play a joke on her? Would they laugh later, thinking of her shivering, alone, among the bones of the dead while they raced to the mall or perhaps to a movie?

Reluctantly, Cricket returned to the old station wagon. The vehicle looked like she felt. Beaten. Used up. If her father knew she had taken the car off the farm, he'd have a fit. No, fifty fits! Right now he was at church, but by noon he would be on his way home. Services were long, beginning at 7:00 A.M. and lasting until almost noon. He would won-der why she claimed sick this morning before they all left for services, and was missing when they got back. She checked her watch. It was only eight. Four hours until Bethany said she would talk to her. She'd forgotten to look under the steps at the store. She could go back and do that now, but dodging people at the orchard would be tough. Someone would talk.

Cricket drove slowly toward the orchard, a plan forming in her mind. She'd gone this far and approached the girl. She had to see this through.

"It's gone!" said Nam angrily, pacing her perfectly pink bedroom. "Gone, gone, gone!"

Bethany and Tillie exchanged glances. "*Now* what's missing?" asked Tillie.

"My amber necklace!"

Today, Nam was dressed entirely in powder blue. Powder-blue drawstring pants with a gauzy tunic top to match, powder-blue shoes, blue eyeliner, and blue dots on her cheek in some sort of crazy design.

"I hope that stuff on your face washes off," said Bethany. Even Nam's eyes were blue. *Blue?* Bethany rubbed her forehead so as not to stare. Nam was like one big, huge, powder-blue sky. *And I have to be seen out in public with this person,* thought Bethany wryly.

Tillie's dark eyes grew wide. "Did you get contacts to match your outfit?"

"What of it?" snapped Nam.

"Well, nothing. It's just that your eyes are such a pretty green . . . and I thought you were going to try to save some money."

"Yeah," said Bethany. "I asked you about those credit cards before. You're not in over your head, are you? You know, I heard on the stock market channel the other day that kids our age will have to save three million dollars over their lifetime just to prepare for retirement."

Nam made a face. "I should have known something else would be stolen. I've been learning astrology, and I've got three transiting squares becoming exact today. I shouldn't even be going out of the house!"

Tillie raised an eyebrow.

"You said something about astrology the other day. Are you teaching yourself, or is someone helping you?" asked Bethany.

Nam made a harumphing sound. "As if you don't know. Ramona is helping me, of course!" She twirled around her bedroom like the bluebird of spring.

Too bad it's the wrong season, thought Bethany.

"How come she's not teaching us?" asked Tillie.

"Because," said Nam, flouncing down at her thoroughly pink vanity, "Ramona says we each have to learn a specialty. I chose astrology." She picked up a purple binder off the floor and fanned the pages. "See? There's a site on the Internet where you can cast charts. I put the information in, and violà!" She puckered her small mouth. "It takes awhile to learn, and I've got a long way to go. What did you guys pick?"

Bethany and Tillie sat totally still. Finally, Bethany said, "She never said anything to us about a specialty."

Tillie shook her head. "Nope, not a word."

Nam began brushing her black hair, looking at the girls through the reflection in the vanity mirror. "Maybe it's because Tillie's so good at the cards. She doesn't need to pick anything."

"But what about me?" asked Bethany. "What am I good at?"

Tillie patted her shoulder. "You're the leader of Witches' Night Out. Learning how to govern a group isn't easy. And you have that healing touch."

Her comments didn't make Bethany feel any better. True, she did run the coven, but that didn't really seem like much. And, to run the coven, she had to be as educated as those in the group on all aspects of magick and occult study. Did Ramona think that Bethany wasn't ready to learn any of those things?

Nam finished brushing her hair and pulled various glossy strands through colorful blue butterfly clips. "What are we going to do today? Go to the mall?" she asked, turning around with a hopeful expression on her face. "I feel like orange!"

"Bleck!" said Tillie.

"Actually," said Bethany, standing up and pulling on last year's winter jacket, "we're going to Cedar Crest Cemetery. I've made a leadership decision!"

"Oh, blast," whispered Tillie, "I don't like the sound of this."

"Hey, you're the one that told her we'd meet her," replied Bethany. "What was up with that? Especially after what Ramona said."

Tillie looked at the carpet sheepishly. "I can't stand to turn someone away who really needs help."

"If you're the leader, Bethany, how come Tillie is the one that said we would go?" asked Nam.

"Can it, Nam," growled Tillie.

"Point well taken," said Bethany, "but if Tillie gave her word, then the rest of us have to back her up. It doesn't matter who's the leader. A Witch is as good as her word."

"I know where we could go!" said Nam, obviously trying her best not to hear the present conversation.

Tillie looked at her suspiciously. "Where?"

"The mall!"

Bethany ran her fingers through her hair and leaned on her knees. "We are going to the cemetery."

"I'll just stay here. Look for my necklace," said Nam, carefully avoiding Bethany's gaze.

Tillie grabbed her by the arm. "No, you don't. If Bethany says we're going to the cemetery, then we're going."

Nam jerked her arm out of Tillie's grasp. "But you said we were going! Why don't *you* go to the cemetery and Bethany and I will go to the mall?"

Tillie growled.

"Okay, okay!" said Nam. "What's this about, anyway?"

"We'll explain it on the way there. I warn you, you're not going to like it," said Tillie.

Nam stuck out her lower lip. "Somehow I thought you'd say that. Will I need a baseball bat? Every time we go to strange places, I'm the one who needs protection! I still think we'd be better off going to the mall!"

"We're off!" said Bethany, marching down the stairs.

"To the mall!" cried Nam.

"Put a sock in it," growled Tillie.

In order for this to work, thought Cricket, *I'll have to be seen by some of the employees, like I'm feeling better now and out here working. At least Alice doesn't work today, she's the only one I don't want to run into. If I use the dirt road to the north rather than the main highway, I should be able to get out to the cemetery without much trouble. I could take the access road through the orchard but there are too many employees living in the cottages along there.*

She turned the station wagon into the store driveway and parked, thought better of it, and pulled around to the back beneath the overhanging branches of the big willow. With the relatively mild weather so far, the willow still had some of its leaves. Not really cover, just light camouflage. The store itself wouldn't be open until one. The best employee to talk to would be Clarence. He was always in the background somewhere.

The store, the garage, and the shed were deserted. Cricket checked her watch. It was only 9 o'clock.

Maybe Clarence decided not to come in to work after all. She circled around the porch and got down on her hands and knees, peering into the gloom underneath. There was something odd back there in the corner.

"You look like you're snoopin' more than you're workin'," came the familiar slow drawl of Clarence's voice.

Cricket jumped, banging her head on the porch step. Her brain cramped and her mouth hung open for the second time that day.

"Better shut your jaw or the flies'll get in there," remarked Clarence, setting down a bushel of apples. He took off his green and orange Bindart's baseball cap and scratched his gray head. "'Course, it's a mite cold fer flies today. What're you doin' under there?"

Cricket snapped her lips together and tried to compose herself. "I thought I saw a critter."

"Uh-huh. How come you ain't at church?" asked Clarence, replacing the hat.

"Didn't feel well," mumbled Cricket, kicking her heel into the thick crust of driveway shale. The stones grumbled under her boot.

Clarence made a funny noise in his throat, an I-don't-believe-you sound.

"But I'm feeling much better now," Cricket said, a little too quickly. "After I stock the store, I thought I'd go out on the north ridge and check the fencing. Deer season starts soon and Daddy doesn't want any poachers on the property. I've seen several in the orchard the past few days. Deer, I mean."

Clarence didn't look convinced of either her quick recovery or her explanation of where she was planning to go. "Don't you normally run the store with Leslee on Sundays?"

Cricket nodded. "She won't mind, not if I stock everything before I go. I'll leave a note on the door. I've done it before." This, actually, was not a lie.

"Uh-huh. You taking the golf cart?"

Cricket brushed a strand of copper hair out of her eyes. It was hard to look straight at Clarence and lie. He was such a nice old man. "No," she said slowly, looking at the ridge, as if she intended to go there. "I think I'll take the station wagon."

"Like ye did this morning?"

Cricket felt the air stop in her chest, as if she'd forgotten how to breathe. "This morning?" she squeaked.

"Don't worry," said Clarence. "I ain't gonna tell. You lit out of here right after sunup. You better be careful," he admonished, waving his finger at her. "Your daddy finds out you've been sneaking off the property, there'll be hell to pay. I hope you remembered to eat your breakfast," he said, tossing her an apple with a flick of the wrist, surprisingly quick for his age.

Cricket caught it and smiled.

He picked up the bushel of apples and started to walk away, but then turned. "He's only trying to protect you, though I think he's going overboard, myself. However, he is your father. He's trying his best the only way he knows how. He don't mean to cause no harm."

She almost said, "His fear hurts us," but thought better of it. Clarence was right, but that didn't make her feel any better about her life, or what was going wrong at the orchard. Cricket tossed the apple in the air and caught it. She was hungry, but when you're raised in an orchard, who wants fruit?

Chapter 7

"This was a dumb idea," said Tillie, shivering in her dirty champagne coat as the noon sun lost itself in a heavy shroud of gray clouds, creating a surreal, shadowless veneer to the cemetery.

Nam drew her powder-blue coat collar tight around her throat, her dark hair flicking around her face like black sparks in the aching-to-be-winter breeze. "I absolutely agree. A dumb idea! At least the mall would be a lot warmer!"

"There's a food court at the mall," lamented Tillie.

"Why'd you pick the graveyard?" asked Bethany.

"I don't know," answered Tillie. "I wasn't sure how much you were going to tell Ramona, so this is the only place I could think of that Ramona might not see us."

"Why, because it's a graveyard?" asked Bethany. "Get real, Tillie. Ramona collects grave dirt for her spells all the time. I'm sure she comes here more than most normal people." She flapped her arms up and down like a giant bird, trying to move to stay warm.

Nam sniggered.

"Everyone's gotta be a critic," said Tillie.

Nam leaned forward, wrapping her arms around herself. "I bet she won't show up. I betcha!"

"Don't be ridiculous," snapped Tillie. She turned to Bethany. "What's with you? Yesterday you were so hot to do a good deed. Today you're chicken. Bawk-bawk." Tillie flapped her arms, mimicking Bethany.

Bethany glared at her. "You weren't the one staring at the business end of a shotgun."

Nam looked around the cemetery. "I should have brought my baseball bat. You didn't say anything about a gun until we got in the car to come here. I can't believe you told that Cricket girl that you'd meet her here." She looked at her matching blue Guess wristwatch. "Where is she, anyway? It's a quarter past twelve. I thought you told her to meet us here at noon? I'm mad at you guys, you know. You went out there last night and didn't say a word to me."

Tillie looked uncomfortable. "We just thought that you wouldn't want to go."

"You were right," said Nam, tapping her foot without realizing it was on a grave. Tap-tap-tap. "But I would have gone anyway. We're a team." Tap-tap-tap went her little powder-blue foot.

"Hey, you fussed about coming here today," bickered Tillie.

"So I complained," said Nam. "Just because I voice my own opinion doesn't mean I'll let you guys wander around without me! Can we leave now, pleeeease?" Tap-tap-tap.

Bethany shook her head firmly. "No. She might have trouble getting away. We'll wait a little longer."

"You know," said Tillie, a mischievous glint in her eyes, "there's an old custom in New Orleans that if you knock on someone's grave three times you'll wake them up. Then, all you have to do," she leaned toward the headstone, "is leave three Xs on the gravestone, like this!" Tillie made three small invisible marks on the stone. "'Course, it works better if you have chalk or crayon."

Nam's contact-blue eyes grew rounder than a computer trackball. "That's not funny, Tillie!" she screamed, jumping from the grave and moving further onto the path, eyeing the plot suspiciously out of the corner of her eye. "Those bushes over there give me the creeps," she said. "What are they, anyway?"

"They're not bushes, they're trees," said Bethany absently. "Yew trees. The symbol of the dead."

Cricket looked at the clock in the store, her frustration mounting. After she talked to Clarence, why hadn't she gone to work in the shed or the garage? Why had she come in here? She knew why—she had to stock for Leslee. And then Alice wandered in.

Quarter past twelve and she couldn't get Alice to shut up or go home. Tad-this and Tad-that. Cricket was sure that Tad was messing around with Alice. No one could be this infatuated. She smiled, her teeth grating. "Yes, I'm sure he's fine. Asked about you? Well, he's been pretty groggy. They doped him up after the surgery, you know. . . . about Janet? Why would he ask about her? Transferring to another school? Your school? No, I had no idea. . . . Janet is lending you books? What books? Fine, then. Don't tell me."

During the last sixty minutes, Cricket was informed of how Alice tried to get into the hospital this morning to see Tad, but Cricket's dad and sister were there and wouldn't let her in the room. That meant that they'd left church early, which would be almost unheard of. She hoped they wouldn't be home too soon. If she could just get rid of Alice!

". . . weird, don't you think?" asked Alice.

"What?" replied Cricket, realizing too late that she wasn't listening to a word Alice said.

"Those girls your father fired yesterday? Bethany Salem? That Witch girl," she ended, screwing her heavy lips in an unpleasant expression. "She probably cast a spell on Tad. They do that, you know. They cast love spells."

"I believe," answered Cricket, "the correct adage is 'judge not that ye be judged,' and why would any one of them be interested in Tad? He never met them until yesterday."

Alice sniffed, her nose in the air, her eyelids collapsing to cat-slits. "I have it from a very good source that they're involved in unsavory activities, like killing animals for sacrifice! You all are just like my family here, I couldn't very well let people like that close to the Bindarts!"

Cricket shook her head. How could Alice make such a ridiculous accusation? Cricket followed the stories in the local papers about Bethany and her friends. The details were sketchy because they were minors, but the articles implied that the girls were instrumental in solving those murder cases, which was why Cricket wanted so badly to speak to them. She had to show Bethany that thing she found under the steps this morning, and maybe they could figure out who left the dead rabbits. She was sure someone was snooping around on the property on a regular basis. Not the employees, either. She'd seen a black Bronco just after midnight. No one here that she knew of drove one.

Cricket felt sick to her stomach. She wished Alice would go find a time warp and never return. She rolled the apple Clarence gave her this morning across the counter, letting it mix with those on the display. She wasn't hungry.

Alice snatched the apple. "Don't put that there. You've been playing with it and probably bruised it." She set the apple under the counter. "Are you sure you don't want it?"

Cricket shook her head.

"I'll just leave it under the counter. Maybe you'll be hungry for it later. We don't want to waste good product, do we?"

Cricket wanted to gag.

"So where is she?" demanded Nam. "It's twelve thirty!"

"Just a few more minutes," wheedled Bethany. She handed Nam the keys to her car. "If you're cold, go warm up the Camaro. I got a new CD last week. The Dixie Chicks."

Tillie feigned barfing sounds.

Bethany pinched her nose with her fingers. "We can't all love Beethoven, you know."

"I've been thinking," said Tillie, "about what Ramona said."

"Ramona says a lot of things," replied Bethany absently.

"About a price to pay and all that. Maybe we're being too hasty."

"Isn't this contemplation a bit after the fact?" asked Bethany.

Tillie shivered against the cold. "I think we made a big mistake. We should have at least looked at the cards, or done some meditation, or even asked around."

"That would have been the smart thing," snapped Bethany.

"You're mad at me."

"A little," sighed Bethany. "I'm supposed to be the leader. I should make the decisions on what our group does."

"Why didn't you say something sooner?"

Bethany shrugged. "Because we're friends, not just Witches, and not just a group. We've been through some tough times together. If I acted like a jerk because I wanted to be big cheese, then what kind of person would I be?"

"You think this is a bad idea, helping Cricket, don't you?"

"We said we'd talk to her. There's still time to back out. Honestly? I don't know how I feel about helping her. I want to be a good person and lend a hand. I took the oath of service just like you, but I've learned Ramona doesn't give her advice lightly. Well, most of the time." She giggled, then sobered. "I guess we'll just take it one step at a time."

"If we wait much longer," said Tillie, "people are going to wonder what we're doing here." She nodded her head toward an older couple placing flowers on a grave. "They've already looked in our direction twice. Dimes to dollars when they leave they'll stop at the cemetery office. We're going to have to go soon."

Bethany nodded. "Yeah. You're right. If she was going to show up, she'd be here by now."

"And all this time I thought you were waiting for me!" said a male voice from behind the bank of yew trees.

Both girls whirled. "Sidney!"

Alice simply would not budge. *Why didn't I hustle her out the door as soon as I realized she was here?* wondered Cricket angrily. She wanted to pick Alice up by the scruff of her coat and fling her out into the parking lot. *A quarter to one,* she thought miserably. *I'm sure they're gone by now.*

"I guess I'll go," said Alice.

The phone rang, startling Cricket off the stool. Her foot caught on a rung and sent it crashing to the wooden planking of the store as she reached for the phone. "It's for you," she said, moving to hand the receiver to Alice.

Alice's face filled with hope. "Is it Tad?"

"No. Some girl. Her voice is familiar but I couldn't place it. She sounds like she's talking with her hand partly over the receiver."

Alice suddenly snatched the receiver from Cricket's hand, her hand slightly shaking. "Yes, yes," she said, turning her back to Cricket and lowering her voice, which was ridiculous because the store was empty and she was less than two feet from the counter. "I got that. The supplies. Yes, that, too. What do you mean you—," she turned and looked quickly at Cricket. "Never mind. We'll discuss it later."

Alice hung up the phone, then tucked her purse under her arm. "I've got to go. Maybe I can get in to see Tad. Do you mind if I take that apple?" She stepped around the fallen stool to reach the fruit.

"Help yourself," said Cricket, picking up the stool and shoving the apple in Alice's hand. She held her breath as she watched Alice slowly clomp down the wide porch steps and meander over to her car. Her spiky blonde hair glittered in the sunlight. The girl turned. "Did you hear that?" she called.

Cricket, standing at the open door, cocked her head. Wind in the trees, a plane overhead, and a few birds. What was there to hear? "What?" she yelled from the doorway.

"A violin," said Alice. "No. A fiddle. Plain as day. You can't hear it?"

Cricket shook her head, just wishing Alice would go. For what seemed like hours, Alice stood in the lot, looking back at the store.

Cricket retreated into the store, hoping that if she acted like she was busy, Alice would just forget the music and shove off. "Please don't let Alice come back here," she whispered to the closed door. Alice finally turned, slowly getting into her car. She adjusted the rearview mirror and sat there, playing with her hair and makeup. Cricket watched the girl with frustration mounting to hysteria. Alice finally maneuvered her car out of the lot, stopping twice to fumble with something on the front seat. Cricket watched the road until Alice's car was completely out of sight. With a little yelp of relief she scribbled a note to her sister, hastily taped the paper to the front door, then flew around to the back where, thankfully, she'd thought to park the station wagon after running into Clarence.

For the hundredth time, Cricket wished that Alice Clement would just drop dead.

Chapter 8

I thought you were staying in New York City until after Thanksgiving!" exclaimed Bethany, hugging Sidney tightly. He was dressed in a tan cable-knit sweater and matching khakis. A blue jean jacket lined with sheepskin hung over his shoulder.

"My father insisted that I have Thanksgiving dinner at home. Mom stayed with my sister. It doesn't matter much to me. This way I can spend more time with you," he said, nuzzling her neck.

Bethany blushed, her stomach giddy.

"Cut it out, you guys," said Tillie. "We're in public, and those old geezers over there will drop dead on the spot if you keep that up."

"At least they're in the right place for it," shot back a smiling Sidney. He was letting his dark hair grow long, secured at the nape of his neck with a leather thong. "So, really, what are you guys doing here?"

"We're waiting for Cricket Bindart," said Tillie. "Nam's toasting her toes in the car. We were just about ready to leave. She's an hour late. I don't think she's going to show. How did you know we were here?"

"They were right," muttered Sidney, "again."

"Who was right?" asked Bethany, leading him back to her car.

"Not important," said Sidney, looking over her shoulder. "I think that girl you were waiting for has just showed up. Bindart of Bindart's Farm and Orchard?"

"The same."

They watched as a rusting and dented station wagon screeched to a halt, and a breathless Cricket jumped out of the car. "I was so afraid you'd gone!" she said, turning to look behind her. A black Bronco slowed at the entrance of the cemetery, then accelerated quickly down the road. "I'm sure I was followed."

"By who?" asked Bethany.

"I don't know," said Cricket, her eyes haunted by some inner anxiety Bethany could not fathom. "That's part of what I wanted to talk to you about."

Large, soft flakes of snow began to fall. "We can't stand out here while you tell us," said Bethany. "We've been waiting outside for an hour and we're just about frozen solid."

"I'm really sorry," said Cricket, wringing work-worn hands. "I tried to get away, but Alice . . ."

"Alice the Malice?" asked Bethany.

Cricket nodded. "But Alice was hanging around. It took forever to get rid of her. I'm so glad you didn't leave! No one can see me talking to you," said Cricket, looking around yet trying to shrink into her own coat. "Can't we go back to your house?"

Bethany shook her head. "Our housekeeper is there."

"My dad's home," said Sidney. "No can do if you don't want anyone to know where you are. My dad knows your father. He's the bank president that holds the loan on your dad's property."

Cricket stepped back, as if thinking to bolt to her car.

"My mother's home with my little brother, and it seems like she knows everyone in the tri-county area, and Nam's house is like Grand Central Station," replied Tillie.

"There's an abandoned barn on my property," said Cricket uneasily, looking at Sidney. "Sometimes my brother and I go there just to get away from everybody. I've got a Coleman stove and some camping supplies. I haven't been out there since it got cold, but I'm sure the stuff is still there. Do you mind going to the barn? It's not terribly close to my house. No one should bother us." She grimaced. "It's not that I don't like you or anything. It's just that my father is very protective and he doesn't know I left the property. I usually have to ask permission."

"And you didn't," said Sidney.

"No."

"Sure, why not," said Tillie. "We can go out to the barn. As long as you've got some munchies."

"On a fruit farm?" laughed Cricket. "We've always got something in season, but I think I have some potato chips and hot chocolate mix in the barn."

"It's a go for me," Tillie replied.

"Where'd you park your car, Sid?" asked Bethany.

"I walked."

Bethany looked at him strangely. "Okay, then pile in with the rest of us."

Bethany carefully followed Cricket's station wagon along the rutted dirt road, worrying more than once as the undercarriage of the Camaro bounced along a pothole or two. Thick, fuzzy snowflakes kissed the windshield, but the snow didn't seem to be laying.

"Geez," said Tillie, hanging over the seat. "This place is really out in the sticks!"

"Anyplace short of Market Square in Cedar Crest is the sticks to you, Tillie," said Nam. "In China, you can walk for days without seeing civilization. In China, you'd be lucky to even have a car. It's funny how different countries can be."

"I'm not going to have a car shortly," said Bethany, "if I don't get a job. As of today my savings account is empty, and as of next week, my car payment is due. If I don't pay my cell phone bill soon they're sure to turn it off."

They rounded a sharp bend. Everyone in the car gasped.

"I thought she said this barn was abandoned?" asked Nam. "The place looks almost brand-new!"

"Yeah. I expected to see . . . well . . . a broken-down barn," said Sidney.

"Don't you guys ever listen to gossip?" asked Tillie. "Old Man Bindart is loaded!"

"Come to think of it," said Sidney, his eyes looking skyward as if he was trying to retrieve information from his mental filing system, "I do remember my dad talking about the Bindart holdings, but not that he has a lot of money. Just the opposite. I think he's going to lose this farm."

"Your dad should know," said Tillie. "After all, he is the president of the bank. That would be a shame if the family lost the farm. This barn is beautiful! Think of all the horses they could have!"

Cricket got out of her car. "Over here," she called as they followed her. "There's a side door."

Inside, Tillie whistled, peering through the gloom. "Why, there's a stage over there!"

Cricket waved her hand. "Oh, when my grandfather was alive they had barn dances here for the employees and the locals. He loved to entertain in a big way. Everybody in the area loved him. At Halloween he would dress up as the headless horseman and chase after the school buses on his favorite black stallion. The kids thought it was fantastic."

"That was your grandfather?" exclaimed Tillie. "Wow!"

Cricket nodded. "That all stopped when he died, though. We don't even keep horses anymore," she said, finishing with a sigh. "Funny," she said, pointing to the cement floor. "There's an oil spot here."

She bent down to check it out. "Looks like someone put kitty litter over the stain, trying to soak up the oil. That's strange. We don't park any of the farm vehicles in this barn." She shrugged. "But I've not been in here for awhile. What do I know?"

"Your dad wasn't into doing the same thing?" asked Bethany. "The Halloween stuff, I mean."

"No," said Cricket, walking over to an old horse stall. She flipped the edge of a black tarp, exposing several camping chairs, a Coleman stove, a cooler, a small table, and a few Coleman lanterns. "You see, Bindart Farm belongs to my mother. She's the Bindart. When my parents were married, my grandfather insisted that the name change be the other way around, and my father was forced to change his last name. My dad never forgave him for it."

"Native American Indians traced their lineage through the mother," said Sidney, "and so did the ancient Celts. I can't see where it's all that big of a deal."

"Tell that to my father," said Cricket. She picked up a lantern, turned on the gas, and carefully lit the glass housing with a long-handled match. She shook the match out and set the lantern in the center of the circle of teens. Its warm light helped to brighten the ominous conversation. "The family used to camp out, too, but we don't do that anymore, either." She rummaged in an old trunk. "That's funny," she said. "I was sure I'd left some snacks in this trunk. I like to come out here to be alone. To read. Sometimes just to think. Empty! Huh! Maybe Tad was in here, but he doesn't particularly like the barn." She struck a long match and lit two of the lanterns. "There, at least we can see. Have a seat, folks!"

"What? No food?" pouted Tillie, sitting on one of the chairs.

"I guess introductions are in order," said Bethany as they circled around Cricket. "This is Nam Chu, Tillie Alexander, and my boyfriend, Sidney Bluefeather. I'm Bethany Salem, but I guess you already know that."

Cricket nodded. "I'm sorry to be so mysterious, but I was heartsick when I heard Dad fired you yesterday. I couldn't believe it when I discovered you were working here. I thought I could finally talk to someone who could help. I've been saving the newspaper clipping about that double homicide you helped solve last month. It was like I knew when I cut it out that you could help."

Bethany and Tillie exchanged worried glances. Nam looked over her shoulder. "This place is spooky."

Cricket smiled. "Sort of, I guess. But I've spent so much time here, I don't notice."

"I've got three squares aspecting my natal chart today. Are you *sure* there's no one else here?" quipped Nam.

Cricket looked more than confused. Tillie rolled her eyes. "Don't mind her; her brain's at the mall."

"Maybe *your* beads are too tight at the roots," retorted Nam.

Tillie adjusted herself, leaning her back against the stall, ignoring Nam. "So what's the big secret? Why couldn't you talk to us out in the open?"

Cricket dropped her eyes. "Oh. Well. You see, my brother and I? We're home-schooled because my father feels that outsiders are a bad influence. He's very strict about who we talk to. I'd be in a lot of trouble if he knew you were here."

"Oh, great," said Tillie. "You mean if he walks in, we're all mincemeat."

Cricket sighed. "He'd just tell you to leave, but he wouldn't be very nice about it. He's been this way ever since my grandpa died. It's as if part of him died, too. It's funny. They didn't really like each other, in fact I think it would be safe to say they tolerated each other, but they both adored my mother and they both loved the farm. Odd, isn't it, how a person or thing can bring two opposite personalities together?"

"What about your mother?" asked Nam. "Doesn't she have anything to say about who you can and can't see?"

Cricket looked around uncomfortably. "My mother stopped talking the day after Grandpa died. My sister, Leslee, sort of took over the mothering part in the family. That was two years ago." She looked at their expressions, then said quickly, "It's okay. She's nice and stands up for Tad and me. Most of the time."

"So you're just lonely?" asked Nam, her voice full of sympathy.

"I wish it was so easy," said Cricket, and before she could stop herself she told them everything. About the fire two years ago, her mother not speaking, the dead rabbits, the many accidents on the farm, how most of the employees quit only after a few weeks of employment without any explanation, and the rumors that had begun to surface about the orchard being haunted.

"Martha Owens," she said, "was a migrant worker that came here every year for the past fifteen years. This summer, she disappeared. No one knows what happened to her. Some of the workers thought she went south, but others felt this wasn't possible. There was even talk of something sinister, but nothing ever came of it. Martha was a dedicated and stable employee, or so my sister said. I was heartbroken when she disappeared. She treated us well."

Tillie shifted. "Did you call the police?"

"My father talked to them, but what could they do? No one bothers to trace a migrant worker. I mean, she hadn't committed a crime and there wasn't any evidence that she didn't decide to drift elsewhere." Cricket withdrew the tanglefoot from the safety of her inner coat pocket and laid it on the ground. "And then I found this," she said, "this morning. I think someone has cursed the farm. I remember seeing something like this when I was a kid, and my grandpa laughed, saying it was a homespun curse. He threw it into the creek. I thought, you being Witches," she looked at Sidney oddly, "that you could, you know, do something about it."

"You've been carrying that around in your pocket all day long?" asked Tillie, a tremor in her voice. "Man, you are one dumb chick."

"Tillie! That's not nice!" said Nam, her powder-blue nails fluttering in the murky barn like plastic moths around the Coleman lantern. "She didn't know any better!"

Sidney kicked the tangled wire with the toe of his boot. "Well . . . what is it?"

"It's to make you trip over yourself," said Bethany. "Negative magick." She thought about Ramona's comment that it might be a few months old. "I looked it up last night, but what I found was vague."

"We should give that to Ramona," said Nam. "She'd know what to do with it."

Bethany shook her head. "Ramona told me not to get involved. She won't take kindly to the fact that I ignored her advice, especially when she's usually right, as you well know."

Nam shifted uncomfortably.

"Who's Ramona?" asked Cricket.

"My housekeeper and watchdog for my father," explained Bethany. "She's also into Hoodoo and tries her best to keep me out of trouble."

Cricket's eyes widened, but all she said was, "Oh."

"So what do we do with it?" asked Sidney. "And who do you think put it under the steps?"

Cricket shook her head. "I have no idea. No one I know even dabbles in magick around here. My father forbids it."

"Because of his religion?" asked Tillie.

"No, because of my grandfather."

Tillie looked over at Nam irritably. "What is your problem? You've been squirming over there for ten minutes."

Nam blushed, her thin chin dipping. "Uh, do you have a restroom here?"

Cricket laughed. "Sure. Up by the stage. The door is marked." She handed the lantern over to Nam. "Take this with you so you can see."

Nam hurried toward the front of the stage, the lantern casting crazy shadows on the barn walls as she toddled along.

"When Nam leaves, our whole world goes dim," said Tillie.

Bethany laughed.

Sidney stretched out his legs and put his arm around Bethany. She smiled inwardly.

Cricket was very pretty and, for a moment, Bethany worried the girl might take too much of an interest in him. She chided herself and picked up the questioning. "What about your grandfather?"

"It's not that big of a deal," said Cricket. "He was a Pow-Wow artist—sort of a faith healer that works magick. When he died, my father burned everything. His notes, papers, diaries . . . even his bed. My father thought he could keep the fire under control, but it got out of hand. He never figured out how. He was sure he'd put it out, but in the night it flared up and took out several buildings, a whole stand of pear trees, and the barn next to the house. A lot of animals died. One worker was severely burned. It was horrid. I think my father secretly feels grandpa caused the fire from beyond the grave as some sort of revenge, but my grandfather wasn't like that at all. He would never do anything to hurt the family, and since that fire, we've been miserable in a lot of ways." She took a breath and sighed deeply, as if finally relieved to drag her family's emotional baggage into the light.

"My older sister, Leslee," she continued, "swore for months that someone was sabotaging our equipment, but my father wouldn't believe her until he surprised someone in the equipment shed not too long ago."

"Did they catch the person?" asked Bethany.

Cricket shook her head. "No. Whoever it was got away. I feel like I'm living inside a Dali painting," she answered. "My brother, Tad, you met him yesterday," she said, looking at Nam, "has been skipping his chores, hours at a time, and doesn't come in till late at night. He won't tell me where he is or what he's doing. I think he's dating some local girls and doesn't want my father to find out. Leslee is acting queer, too. She takes a lot of overnight trips, claims it's for business, but neither my grandfather nor my dad ever had to do that. Since the fire my mother won't speak to anyone. She spends most of the time in her room watching westerns on her VCR. I feel like my entire life is coming apart!"

Tillie shook her head. "And I thought Nam's family was dysfunctional." Her hand flew over her mouth. "Sorry, Cricket, that was rude."

"It's okay. I'd be the first to admit it, but the mutilated rabbits? That was the last straw. I've got to figure out what's going on. This whole mess is just getting too scary."

Bethany and Tillie looked at each other. Tillie moved her head, the beads in her hair whispering in the quiet barn. "How did you find the tanglefoot?"

Cricket sucked on her lower lip. "Last night I locked up the store and turned out the lights, but I forgot something in the cooler room. That's where we keep some of the perishables and the cut flowers from the garden when they are in season. Anyway, when I returned from the cooler, I saw Bethany trying to get something out from under the steps."

"It was you in the window!" said Bethany.

"Yes, but I couldn't say anything to you because I saw Leslee coming across the parking lot. I decided just to watch. I heard her ask you to come back to work. Could you? I know it's a lot to ask. My father isn't the easiest to work for. It's just that I feel like our whole family has an emotional flu, and if I can do something, I could fix it. Please say you'll help. I don't think I can figure this all out by myself."

"Um, we haven't really made up our minds," stalled Bethany, ignoring Tillie's insistent eyes.

"How do you know we didn't put the tanglefoot under the steps?" said Tillie. "I mean, we could have been mad at your father for firing us."

Cricket stared at them dumbly. "I guess I never thought about it that way." For a moment, fear flickered in her mystical blue eyes.

Tillie laughed. "Don't worry. In fact, Bethany found it yesterday afternoon when Alice demanded she clean under the steps. She was going to get rid of it, but then the accident happened. We thought we'd come back last night and do our witchy good deed."

"And got caught in the act," said Bethany.

"Sounds to me like you've got more than one mystery brewing here," remarked Tillie.

Sidney leaned forward a bit, forcing Bethany to adjust her shoulders, "About that fire—"

A loud crash from the stage area echoed through the barn, followed by a high-pitched, feminine scream.

"Nam!" shouted Tillie, jumping to her feet and running toward the stage. "Nam! Are you all right?"

Chapter 9

They found Nam huddled at the bottom of the dusty stage steps, mumbling.

"What's she saying?" cried Cricket.

"Something about three squares," said Sidney, pulling Nam to her feet. "Are you okay?"

Nam nodded, her lower lip sucked in so far under her front teeth that she looked like a candidate for lower dentures. "Somebody jumped me!" she said, her tiny fists balled next to her cheeks. "He's over there. In the corner!" She held out a shaking hand, her powder-blue nails jittering. "I knew I should've brought my baseball bat!"

Cricket rescued the lantern from the floor and started to laugh.

"What's so funny?" snapped Nam, her cheeks colored with indignation. "That guy attacked me!"

Cricket swallowed a giggle, the sound burbling in her throat. She walked over to the corner and held up a plastic pumpkin head with skeleton arms. "You mean this guy? It's just a Halloween prop. My grandfather sponsored a haunted house exhibit for the local fire hall every year. We've got quite a collection of masks, costumes, and other junk."

Bethany and the others couldn't help laughing. "I'm sorry," Bethany apologized, patting Nam's shoulders. "But it is funny. We're talking about curses, a serious fire, and that darned tanglefoot and then you have a run-in with Mr. Pumpkinhead over there. Gave us all a fright."

Nam forced a shaky smile. "Yeah. I guess you're right. But I swear, it came flying out of nowhere and hit me on the head."

Tillie's lips parted in a mischievous grin. "It was probably that ghost from the graveyard. You tapped on his grave and woke him up. Now he's following you."

"That's not funny!" exclaimed Nam, her eyes wider than bottle caps.

Cricket sobered. "So, do you think you guys can help me?" Again, she cast an odd expression at Sidney.

Bethany looked at Cricket sharply, and Cricket didn't miss it.

"I'm sorry," Cricket said, "but I didn't think boys were Witches, and I didn't think Witches had bank presidents for parents."

"'Witch' doesn't mean gender," said Tillie. "Witchcraft is a religious faith. So, we're all Witches, like all Christians are Christians and all Jewish people are Jewish."

"So, you're a Witch, too?" Cricket asked Sidney.

"Absolutely," he replied. "I'm also a member of the Cherokee Nation through my mother. A Ni Wa Yah, Keepers of the Wolf. And no, I won't say anything to my dad. If he thought there was a way to make more money out of this, he'd do it. I love my father, but he is a cold businessman. I don't want him foreclosing on your property any more than you do."

Nam was busily patting her hair. "I think I lost one of my butterfly clips."

Cricket brought the lantern closer as they all started to look on the dusty concrete floor.

"I think I found it," said Sidney, rising slowly.

Later, he would tell them he never felt the blow.

"I can't believe that man hit you," said Bethany, holding an ice pack on the back of Sidney's head as they sat around the Salem's dining-room table.

He winced. "Remind me not to piss off any more farmers."

Nam ran her powder-blue nails along the smooth edge of the table, her face ivory pale. "He said he was sorry that he thought you were an intruder."

"Yeah, right," said Sidney. "We're all standing there and he just happens to hit me from behind. Talk about cowardly."

"You could sue!" said Tillie fiercely.

Bethany shook her head. "And add more problems to the orchard. That guy was just the hired help, supposedly sent out to look for Cricket. I bet she's in a lot of trouble right now because of us."

"It's her own fault," said Tillie icily. "She's the one that invited us there."

"I feel sorry for her," said Nam. "She isn't allowed to associate with people her age. That would be horrible! Don't be too hard on her."

"Too bad we left the tanglefoot," Bethany said. "That little charm certainly seems to be causing a lot of trouble."

Sidney reached into his pants pocket. "I've got it. When Nam screamed, I picked it up. You can kindly get the stupid thing away from me." He dropped the twisted wire on the dining room table. Everyone sat back as it slid a few inches on the slick surface.

Nam looked at the little charm distastefully. "Better get it out of here before Ramona sees it. She'll know what it is right away, and where it came from. She'll be angry you brought it into the house."

"I don't get it," said Sidney, "why should she care?"

"It's one of her house rules. If you think it might be magick, but you're not sure what kind, then you don't bring it in the house. She claims that to do so invites any evil that might be associated with it inside the soul of the family."

"Oh, I never thought of it that way. Where is she, anyway?"

Bethany shrugged. "Your guess is as good as mine. I'm just glad she wasn't standing by the front door this time with the broom. She's not in the house, so maybe she went out for awhile."

They all stared at the mangled wire ball.

Nam chewed her lips pensively. "Do you think the orchard is really cursed?"

"But I swear to you I left a note!" wailed Cricket. She'd never seen her father this angry. Zee stood behind him, expressionless.

"That doesn't explain why those kids were out there in the barn with you. Having a make-out party!" he bellowed, throwing his arms in the air. "Obviously the note was a lie! Zee!" snapped her father.

"Yessir?"

"Clean that barn out. Trash everything."

"Won't be able to get to it until next week," said Zee. "We're too short on help."

A spasm of irritation flicked across Old Man Bindart's face. "Fine. Next week. And next time, ask questions before you clobber something. That kid you hit is the son of the president of my bank. I've already got enough problems, I don't need him suing me or trying to foreclose on this property any sooner than we can help it. If he says anything, you're to say the kid swung first, and he was trespassing on private property."

Zee nodded, an uncomfortable expression on his face. He left the bedroom silently. In the dimness of the hall, standing silently beside the peeling wallpaper,

Cricket could see the frightened eyes of her mother. She turned and scurried away before Cricket could reach out.

"Maybe we should just throw it in running water, like Cricket's grandfather did. I mean, it sounds like he practiced magick. He just laughed and got rid of it. Why can't we do the same thing?" asked Tillie. "Ha, ha, and toss it."

"And what if that's not the right thing to do?" asked Nam. "What if a fish swallows it? Then what? We might do more harm than good."

"Let me think," said Bethany. "Hold on a minute." She raced up to her room and got her magickal journal, where she'd been keeping notes of Ramona's classes, as well as things she'd found in personal study. "Here!" she said, when she returned to the dining room. "Breaking Hexes. We can boil it, urinate on it—"

"Yick!" squealed Nam. "I'm not doing that!"

Tillie laughed. "You would if you were desperate. What else?"

"Soak it in vinegar, or burn it. Let's see. For circular objects . . . is this a circular object?"

"Looks bent to me," said Sidney.

"Funny. For circular objects you are to freeze it, then boil it, then soak in vinegar. That's if you want to keep it."

Nam sucked on her lips. "Why should we want to keep it?"

"I think that's for jewelry," said Tillie. "You know, something valuable that you don't really want to get rid of."

"Oh," said Nam.

"We can't burn it," said Tillie. "It's metal."

"So I guess that leaves soaking it in vinegar," said Sidney. "How long do we soak it?"

Bethany looked over her notes. "For at least twenty-four hours, and then bury the object off of your property, preferably at a legitimate crossroads."

"Is there such a thing as an illegitimate one?" asked Sidney.

"Beats me," replied Bethany. "Okay, gang, let's put this puppy where it belongs. Nam, there's a bunch of canning jars in the basement with lids. Go get one."

"Me? The basement? No way. I've got three—"

Tillie stood up. "Aspecting squares in your natal chart today. Geez, Nam. Come on. I'll go with you."

"Alice," said Leslee, looking unhappily at her younger sister, "it was Alice. Here," she pushed the dinner tray closer to Cricket. "Eat up." Leslee kicked the bedroom door partially shut with her foot.

Cricket sat in the center of her bed, staring at the food. The mashed potatoes and gravy were congealed on the plate. Her stomach turned. "Alice . . . what?"

Leslee ran her hand through the dark-blonde hair at her temple, while her other hand remained hooked in the back of her jean pants pocket. "From what I've been able to gather, Alice drove down the road, then turned around and came back in time to see you tape the note on the door. She took the note, then followed you. She watched you bring those kids back to the old barn, then busted butt to tell Dad that you were having a make-out party, and that it was getting out of hand. She ran into Zee first and spun a mighty tale. He was convinced you were having an orgy in there. I didn't know anything about it until it was over. I'm sorry. I would have stopped her if I could, and I know I could have talked some sense into Zee."

"It doesn't matter." Cricket turned away, her head down. How she hated Alice Clement!

Leslee sighed. "I'm firing Alice tomorrow afternoon. She's more trouble than she's worth, and the register in the store is off again. I counted two hundred dollars missing last week. I can't accuse Alice, but someone is dipping into the till. We sure haven't been having much luck lately."

"I didn't take the money."

"You think I don't know that?" asked Leslee. "It's like the same problem we had last month when I fired that other girl. Even the amount of money missing is in the same denominations."

"Maybe it was Alice all along?"

Leslee shook her head. "Couldn't be. I caught that other girl red-handed."

Cricket didn't reply. At least Alice would be gone, but that didn't fix the damage she'd done.

Leslee paced the room. "Look, I know things have been tough here the past few years. Just hang in there. I'm really trying to lighten Dad up."

"It's not working. He's getting worse. You're lucky, though. You could get out of here. Why don't you? Why do you stay in this horrible place?" asked Cricket, feeling the hysteria build in her throat.

Leslee looked up at the ceiling. "I guess I have a few reasons. You and Tad, to start." Her gaze traveled back to Cricket. "If I left now, then I know things would escalate. Mom couldn't possibly handle him, or even the housework. Besides, I've worked too many years to be thrown out of my inheritance, should there even be one. At the rate things are going around here, we may be out on the street by spring. I lost a whole section of pear trees to blight last summer, and the peaches rotted on the branches because no one wanted to come in to pick them. This farm has a bad rep and migrant workers are historically superstitious."

Cricket nodded glumly. "Maybe that would be a good thing—losing the orchard. Maybe then we could live like everybody else."

Leslee snorted. "I doubt it. Besides, I was hoping to keep the orchard. It would be a great place to raise the baby."

Cricket sat up. "What baby?"

Leslee smiled. "Promise you won't tell?"

Cricket shook her head, eyes wide. "I promise," she whispered.

"I'm pregnant!"

"No!" squealed Cricket, then slapped her hand over her mouth. She slowly removed her fingers. "You can't be! You're not married!"

"Surprise number two," said Leslee. "I've been married for over two years. I wanted to tell you sooner, but Dad surely would have thrown me out."

Cricket practically fainted on the bed. "Who? Who?"

"I can't tell you. Not yet."

Fear clutched at Cricket's chest. "But what about Daddy? If you tell him, he will throw you out! I couldn't bear to be here without you!"

Leslee nodded. "Yeah, I know. As long as I keep my mouth shut, I can stay. Soon, though, I'll have to say something." She patted her stomach. "I've been racking my brain to come up with a way to break the news. If I do have to go, though, we've got a second income. It isn't the greatest, but we could survive. I have a third surprise—"

A dark shadow fell over Cricket's bed. Fearfully, she looked over Leslee's shoulder. "Consider the news broken," said her father.

Leslee's shoulders stiffened. Slowly she turned to face her father.

"Pack your things and get out. I always knew you were nothing more than a tramp."

Leslee stepped back, her thighs bumping into the bed. Cricket sat up on her knees and the entire dinner tray tipped, then slid off the side of the bed in a loud clatter of broken glass. The tin tray bounced, echoing on the hardwood floor.

"You wouldn't dare!" Leslee said, throwing a frightened look at Cricket. "You couldn't! You can't run this place without me!"

Without a moment's warning, he struck her. Cricket watched in horror as her sister's head rocketed to the side and she lost her balance, hitting the back of her skull on the bedpost. Without a murmur she collapsed on the floor, blood oozing across the high polished wood. Cricket's father stepped back, his eyes unfocused and hollow. He looked at his hand as if it didn't belong to him, then turned and left the room.

Chapter 10

Monday morning

*B*ethany was convinced she was still dreaming, as the scene before her could not possibly be a part of everyday reality. She pinched herself, but it really hurt. Finally she asked, "Ramona, what *are* you doing?"

The housekeeper continued to mutter in French as she pushed a large red ball across the kitchen floor with her broom. "And! My vinegar is gone!" she said, hitting the ball with a mighty thrust.

"Yeow!" squealed Bethany as the object hit her in the shin, then rolled underneath the kitchen table. Hecate eyed the ball but didn't touch it, opting not to participate. "What are you trying to do, gear up for the local Hoodoo hockey team?" asked Bethany. That thing was too hard to be a regular ball.

Ramona stood up straight. "You've been up to no good! I know you have. I don't know exactly what you've done, but you definitely brought evil into this house. I can feel it!" She fished the red object out from underneath the table and continued to roll it around the floor, perspiration gathering on her smooth brow.

"What is that?" asked Bethany.

"An onion wrapped in red flannel," Ramona replied, continuing to push the ball around. "It will collect all the evil, and then . . . " She opened the back kitchen door, and with one mighty swipe, sent the ball zooming into the back yard. "One must send it out of the house! Couldn't find my vinegar. Had to have that vinegar to do my spell. Had to go out at six this morning to the convenience store just to get that vinegar!" She held up the broom handle, pulling off a piece of paper secured by a red rubber band, then took a lighter from the pocket of her white smock, held the paper over the sink, and burned it, flushing the ashes down the drain with running water. "The things Ramona has to do just to keep you out of trouble! Get ready for school," she snapped. "Or you'll be late!"

"She did *what*?" asked Tillie, chewing on the barrel of her pencil.

"Stop that!" said Nam, flicking her long, grave-black nails at the pencil. "You can't eat that!" She rooted in her purse. "Here, have some gum." Nam's color for the day gave black a new meaning.

Bethany, Tillie, Nam, and Sidney sat in fifth-mod study hall. The substitute teacher said she didn't mind if they talked quietly.

"Pushed the onion around the kitchen, claiming she was clearing the house of evil. She was mad because the vinegar was gone. I guess we shouldn't have used the whole bottle," said Bethany, "but I wanted to be sure."

"I told you she would know," said Tillie, chewing the gum with gusto. "How come the flavor in gum never lasts very long?"

"She doesn't *know* know," said Bethany. "Her spirits don't seem to give her all the details all the time, thank goodness."

Sidney leaned on his fist, saying nothing.

Tillie's eyelids closed halfway as she eyed Sidney. "That's right, Sid old boy, didn't you tell us at your dedication ceremony that you hear ghosts, too?"

Sidney shifted uncomfortably in his seat, looking around to make sure no one had heard her. "Shush-up about that, Tillie. I don't really want to get into it here."

"Nothing doing," said Tillie. "Isn't that what you said?"

Sidney's jaw stiffened, and he nodded curtly. "Yeah. Sometimes. That's right. Now drop it."

Tillie rolled her eyes. "Aren't we sensitive?"

"Stop it," said Nam, looking from Tillie to Sid. "He's right." She lowered her voice, her green eyes looking like kohl slits. "Not here, and not now. Besides, I wanted to tell you guys that Janet wasn't in school today. I was going to give her a piece of my mind about making that scene yesterday and setting us up with Alice the Malice, but she wasn't here."

"Figures," said Tillie. "Coward. Talk about two-faced! She's always causing problems on the debate team. Maybe she transferred already. That would be a major relief!"

Nam cocked her head and adjusted the collar of her black silk blouse. "It doesn't matter. I've made up my mind to speak to her when she gets back—if she gets back! If not, I just might find out where she lives and give her a piece of my mind!"

"Yeah, right," said Tillie. "Nam the Super Witch. What are you gonna do, hex her with a few aspects?"

Nam sniffed and elevated her small chin. "A lot you know!"

Tillie slapped the desk with her open palm, earning a disapproving glance from the substitute. "You go, girl!" she whispered. "Just give the high-five sign and I'll go with you."

"Did you hear about all the commotion in the ag room this morning?" asked Nam.

Everyone shook their heads.

"Remember the bunny fiasco last week?"

Nods all around.

"What nobody said was that the prize chinchilla rabbits have been missing for over a week. The girl that had them for her project is devastated. The school thought if they kept quiet about it that they'd find out who took them, but the news leaked out this morning."

Everyone at the table sat stone silent.

"You don't think . . . " asked Tillie, her voice trailing off into the quiet study hall room.

Nam's eyes rounded. "That would be horrible! But how could rabbits from here get all the way over to the next county and into Cricket Bindart's mailbox?"

The silence continued. "Maybe we should tell someone," Nam offered.

"If we said something," said Tillie, "they would blame us for it."

"No, they wouldn't!" protested Nam.

Bethany pulled on her earlobe. "Think about it. Cricket didn't tell her parents. Only Tad knows, and he's in the hospital. We have a connection to Bindart's because we worked there on Saturday."

"But they found the rabbits before we worked there."

"Doesn't matter," replied Tillie. "Bethany's right. Guilt by association."

"We can't just sit here and do nothing," complained Nam.

"Fine," said Tillie. "Then let's go back to work there and do some snooping around."

Nam cringed.

"You said you wanted to help," admonished Tillie.

"I don't know, Tillie," said Bethany. "Remember what Ramona told us, plus she was so upset this morning."

"What's with you lately, Bethany?"

"I just don't know if we can make a difference, is all. Maybe we should sit this one out?"

"I agree with Bethany," said Nam. "I'm sure we could find another way to help without going back there to work."

"And you both have come up with fast cash to pay your bills?" asked Tillie.

Neither girl responded.

"I know we can make a difference," said Tillie. "We have before, and we will again. The point is, we have to try. It's not right to sit on the information we have and not do anything about it. It's unethical."

"She's right," said Sidney, who up until this point appeared to have purposefully avoided joining the discussion.

Bethany gave him a dirty look.

"Hey, I'm a member of this group, too," he said. "I vote with Tillie."

"But it isn't you who's supposed to work there," said Bethany.

"Right," said Sidney sheepishly. He sat forward and grinned. "To change the subject, my dad's bank is sponsoring a hayride as part of some loan deal they're running. Bindart's farm is hosting it. Maybe we could do a little snooping. You guys want to come along? It's Wednesday. The night before Thanksgiving."

Cricket remained in her room. No one to talk to. No one to care. No one to hear her sobs. She was sure the house was deserted—had been all day. Where was her mother? Last night Zee took her barely conscious sister away, anger blazing in his eyes. She wanted to call the police, but what would she say? Leslee wasn't here. She had no idea where Zee took her. There wasn't even any blood on the floor. Her mother came in late with a pail of water and floor soap, never uttering a word, never looking up at Cricket. Not even once. Cricket wasn't sure who she hated the most right now—her father, Zee, her mother for not defending her children, Alice Clement for her fat mouth causing all this, or Leslee for getting herself pregnant.

Who was running the store? Surely not her mother, and Alice would be fired when she came in this afternoon. Oh, no! How could Alice be fired if Leslee disappeared?

Cricket's mind just kept running in circles, around and around. Who was Leslee's husband? Was he worried about her? Did he know she was in trouble? Cricket twisted her pillow, damp from hours of weeping, in her cold, swollen fingers. She looked at her fingers strangely. How long had she been doing this? All night? All day? What about the unborn baby? Was it all right? Her sister had been trained in the military. A Marine, for heaven's sake. Why hadn't she defended herself?

But Cricket knew why. Their father had never lashed out at any of them in all these years.

Until now.

She wouldn't have believed it if she hadn't seen it herself.

She groaned a long, low, teeth-clenching wail.

She wished Alice Clement would just wither and die!

This was all her fault!

The door to her bedroom remained open, but she didn't want to go out in that dark hallway. Or down the stairs. Or anywhere.

Bethany waited for Tillie after school, then drove at a leisurely pace toward home. At the last moment, Bethany pushed her foot on the accelerator and sped up, zooming past her house.

"Hey!" shouted Tillie, her head snapping up from an intense search through her backpack. The lip balm slipped from her fingers, rolling onto the carpeted floor of the Camaro. "Why did you do that? Oh, my Goddess! Bethany, there's two police cruisers in your driveway!"

"I know. What do you think I drove by for?"

"Yeah, but something could be wrong! Someone could be hurt. Maybe Ramona. We should go back. I mean, you didn't do anything . . . wrong . . . did you?"

"Don't be ridiculous!"

"Then why did you drive by?"

Bethany's hands shook as she pulled over to the side of the road. "I don't know. I just had this horrible, awful feeling . . . and if it is something bad, I need to calm down, take a deep breath, and get ready to face it. Do you understand?"

"I guess so. It can't be too bad, Bethany. If something was wrong with your father, the NYPD would be here, not the local cops."

"Maybe. Do you have your cards with you?" asked Bethany.

"Yes, but that's silly. We should just go back there and find out."

Bethany was so frightened that her chest tingled with an odd, aching pain. "Just get them out!"

Tillie frowned. "Sure. Sure." She dug the tarot cards out of the side pocket of her backpack. "Okay, now what?"

"You tell me," said Bethany, feeling sick to her stomach. "You're the card reader."

"Aw, shoot."

"What! What is it? Sidney, is it Sidney? My dad? Ramona? Oh, no, not Nam, again!"

"Take a chill pill," said Tillie, concentrating as she laid the cards out on top of her chemistry book on her lap. "Don't rush me. I always make mistakes when people get antsy!"

Okay, Bethany said to herself. *Be calm. Think it, be it. Think it, be it. Okay, okay.*

"It's not your dad or Sidney," said Tillie, waving a court card, "because it's a woman. In fact, I've drawn the Queen of Cups, the Queen of Wands, and the Empress. Huh."

"Who's who?"

Tillie scratched her temple. "I don't think any of them are Ramona. She's usually the Queen of Swords whenever I do a reading. Do you know anyone that's pregnant?"

Bethany shook her head. "No."

"There's swords crossing the Empress, that's who I think is pregnant. Four of swords. Possibly a hospital stay or a recovery of some kind."

Bethany shook her head, confused. "And the others?"

"The Queen of Cups is crossed by the Ace of Swords, the Nine of Swords, and the Ten of Swords. That's bad. Real bad."

"Oh, Holy Mother! And you have no idea who it is?"

Tillie shrugged her shoulders. "It could be anybody, I guess."

"How helpful."

"Hey! I'm not God. I only read cards."

Bethany flapped her hand. "And the last court card?"

"The Queen of Wands is crossed by the Eight of Swords. That's self-imposed imprisonment. That might be Cricket."

"Might be," said Bethany. "I hope nothing bad has happened to her. She seemed like an okay person, but then, with that weird family of hers, anything is possible."

I've experienced this scene before, thought Bethany as she entered the kitchen. One Cedar Crest officer sat at the table drinking herbal tea and eating chocolate-chip cookies, the other stood ramrod straight by the door, a frown heavily creasing his massive forehead. Hecate sat in the corner, his ears semi-flattened, glaring at the bigger officer. *Cats know a jerk when they see one,* thought Bethany.

"As I was saying," Officer Charles smiled, waving a cookie in the air, "Ramona, this is the third time your . . . er . . . charge . . . "

"I prefer to think of her as my adopted niece," said Ramona, smiling back.

"Uh, yes. Niece. Okay then. This is the third time Bethany has been involved in a murder investigation, and although I'm not suspicious, not in the least . . . well, some of the fellows at the station who aren't very sympathetic, to . . . er . . . your religion . . . Wicca, isn't it?" He bit into the cookie. The larger officer looked at him with disgust.

"Murder?" exclaimed Tillie. "What murder?"

"The Queen of Cups," muttered Bethany.

Ramona nodded, her smile frozen in place, her eyes blazing like jet beads. "Bethany practices Wicca, yes."

"The fellows at the station . . . they're not very progressive," continued Officer Charles between munches. "Uh . . . they aren't happy that Bethany is involved . . . again," he finished. "If Carl Salem wasn't a police officer . . . "

"Murder," repeated Tillie. "What murder? Who's been murdered?"

Officer Harrison, the larger cop, turned, setting his stern gaze on the girls, while Officer Charles motioned for them to sit down with the remainder of his cookie. Years ago, before Bethany's father became a detective at the NYPD, both men came often to the Salem house to play poker. Neither appeared to be the fellows she remembered from those long-ago card nights. The fact that she knew them, though, was better than dealing with complete strangers. If she remembered correctly, Harrison was always a poor sport and would throw his cards when he lost the pot. She'd found the two of clubs stuck in the kitchen wainscoting one morning after a late-night game. He wasn't behaving any better now, pulling out the chair and sitting on the edge of it, as if the ladies in the kitchen would pounce should he be so stupid to relax.

A horrid stillness settled over the table. Bethany spoke quietly. "Who has passed away?"

"Murdered," said Harrison. "The question should be, who has been murdered?"

Bethany balked. The man seemed to love that word. She watched him carefully. Lean these days, with cruel lines around his eyes and mouth that weren't there before. Clearly, some bad things had happened to him and she was sure that he used his position in the community to intimidate others. Charles, on the other hand, still looked plump and jovial, just several years older. If she didn't know better, Bethany thought he was gazing at Ramona a little too long. Now this was an interesting twist.

"All right," said Bethany, pointedly ignoring Harrison and turning to face Officer Charles. "Who has been *murdered*?" She elongated the word, hoping Harrison would squirm.

He did, then opened a small notebook, the black cover worn from use. "Alice Clement. Aged 16. One hundred and fifty pounds. Five foot, one inch. Junior at Northern High School. Band member. Short, blonde hair. Blue eyes. Lived at 422 Becker Road, Carroll Township, Adams County. Ring a bell?"

"Yeah, she's shaped like one," muttered Tillie.

Ramona shushed her.

Bethany could only feel shocked. "Alice Clement? The girl that works at Bindart's Orchard?" she asked.

"Yes," said Harrison. "When was the last time you saw her?"

"How did she die?" asked Tillie.

"When did she die?" asked Bethany.

Officer Charles held up his hands. "Ladies! One question at a time, but first, if you please, we'd like you to answer our questions. Unfortunately, we're keeping the nature of the young lady's death confidential for the moment. Now, Bethany, when did you last see Alice Clement?"

"Um. Gee. Let me think. I guess it would have been Saturday afternoon, at the orchard."

"And you haven't seen her since?" asked Officer Charles.

"No."

Harrison leaned forward, his cold eyes picking at her like she was a human sore. "Are you sure?"

Bethany really did not like this man. Her own irritation felt like spiders waltzing down her arms. She shivered internally, but showed nothing of her feelings to this ogre. "Of course I'm sure! Saturday was the first and the last time I ever saw her. I'm not kidding. I never met the girl before that. I think I worked with her for a total of four, maybe five hours. Certainly not long enough to want to kill her!" *Well,* she thought, *not in the literal sense.*

"How about you?" asked Harrison, fixing his gaze on Tillie. "Did you know her?"

Tillie actually grinned. "Yeah, for about five minutes, and enough to learn she wasn't the nicest person in the world!"

Officer Charles took a refill on his tea from Ramona. Harrison refused. He didn't even touch a cookie.

Bethany's brain fidgeted. She wished these two men would just go.

"Strange people," said Harrison, focusing on Bethany. "The Bindarts, I mean. Odd people. Some say religious fanatics. Alice went to their church, you know. With the home-schooling, they definitely wouldn't care for . . . ah . . . the more avant-garde types of people. Say, for instance, Witches."

Bethany could feel herself bristling, but before she could say anything, Tillie spoke up. "Just because they're into home-schooling doesn't mean they're strange," she said. "Sometimes, the way people treat you at school, a kid might like the protective environment of the home. Maybe the parents are afraid of the drugs, and guns, and general nastiness that goes around. I don't think you can really blame them and call them weird just because they want what's best for their kids. My parents talked about it seriously, but they were afraid that my brother and I would somehow be socially impaired." She smiled a perfect Tillie smile. "I've got such a big mouth, though, I don't think that would ever be a problem, but I like cheerleading and swimming, and I don't want to give those things up. Some school systems let the home-schooled kids participate, but many more don't. I know Cedar Crest doesn't. If you are home-schooled in our district, you aren't allowed to participate in after-school sports, or the debate team, or anything. You can't even get a high school diploma from them even though you use their books and have to fill out tons of paperwork just to be allowed to teach your kids yourself, but some parents think it's still worth it because at least, at home, they won't get a phone call saying their kid was shot at school, or put up with incompetent teachers that the administration is afraid to fire because of politics or bad press, or be haunted to the breaking point by bullies, which has absolutely nothing to do with religion and everything to do with safety and quality teaching!"

Bethany's mental jaw dropped, but she kept her mouth physically closed.

Harrison moved uneasily in his chair.

Officer Charles came to the rescue, a slight smile playing around his lips. "Young lady, you should get into politics when you get older, but I think he means, Tillie, even though you were there for a short time, did you see anything odd or unusual?" He looked pointedly at Harrison, then turned back to Tillie. "You see, a while back there was a fire that injured one migrant worker, and the nature of the fire was ruled undetermined. Then, last summer, a migrant worker disappeared. Now, this teenager is dead. All three tragedies are tied to the Bindart farm."

Bethany thought of the tanglefoot and the mysterious fiddle, and how about that car that tried to run them down? None of which she would dare discuss with these guys. Her eyes slid slowly toward Tillie.

"The only thing strange I saw . . . " began Tillie as Bethany held her breath, "is the big dude with the black, bushy beard and coveralls. He could eat a kid for breakfast, no problem."

Ramona leaned forward, her eyes like blazing coals. "Tell me, Officer Harrison, how is it that you have come here, to the home of Carl Salem, to ask your questions? It is obvious that these two girls didn't know the victim personally, save for a few hours on a single day."

Harrison blinked. Officer Charles visibly shriveled back in his chair. Hecate stepped forward, hissing.

Officer Charles recovered, trying his best to give a winning smile. "Why, we had an anonymous tip that Bethany and . . . " he pointed at Tillie, "were involved. Of course we didn't believe it, but since the girls did see Miss Clement shortly before she died, we thought they might have some clue as to her . . . ah . . . demise. I'm sure you understand. I mean, it is our job to ask questions."

"Huh." She looked at the larger officer. "I'd guard your leg, Officer Harrison. Our cat seems to think it's a big drumstick. A turkey drumstick."

Chapter 11

Monday evening

Bethany snuggled in Sidney's arms, the worries about Cricket, the Bindarts, and Alice Clement's death scurrying around the edges of her mind like a pack of hamsters after a box of blueberries. "I missed you," she murmured, trying to push away the troubling thoughts. She'd hardly spent any time with him alone since he came back from the city. They lounged on the family room sofa, a cold rain spitting on the bay windows from blackened skies beyond. The steady sound of soft, rhythmic drums floated through the room.

"What's that noise?" asked Sidney, his eyes barely open as he rested his chin on her head.

"Ramona," said Bethany. "When Dad's away, she stays in the upstairs guestroom. He bought her a compact disk player for her birthday."

"Are you sure she's not up there doing something strange and banging her own drum?"

Bethany giggled. "I wouldn't put it past her."

"Sounds kinda neat."

"Yeah."

He stroked her hair. "So the cops came around this afternoon?"

Bethany sighed. "I didn't like Alice, but I haven't a clue who might want to hurt her."

"Do you think Cricket knows?" asked Sidney.

Bethany could feel a bit of jealousy rearing its ugly head, shoving bits of flame into her veins. "About Alice? Probably. I mean, I'm sure the cops were over there." She dismissed Cricket with a wave of her hand, hoping Sidney wouldn't say anything else about the girl.

"The police may have gone to the Bindart farm, but that doesn't mean that they talked to her, or that her father even told her," theorized Sidney. "Maybe we should try to contact her."

"How? Call? There's no way that family would let us speak to her."

"I see your point. We couldn't just go over there and knock on the door, either. Especially since you didn't take Leslee up on the job offer."

Bethany bit her lip and didn't reply, hoping the subject of Cricket would go away. They fell silent, listening to the sleeting rain claw against the window.

"I'm sorry I snapped at Tillie today," whispered Sidney. "But what I see is personal, and when I was little, the family made fun of me. Not my mother, but the rest of them. It got to be so painful that I just sort of shut up about it."

Bethany, head softly resting on his chest, listened to the steady beat of his heart. She'd been seeing

Sidney seriously for only a few weeks. In a way, she wanted him to open up, to talk to her, but a part of her was really afraid. True, Joe, her old boyfriend, was gone, dead. Buried. But he'd taken up her whole life—ate her alive, in a way—and she wasn't sure if she wanted to go back to something like that ever again. Life was so full of promises . . . and broken trusts. She licked her lips. Her skin tingled when his fingers touched her cheek. So far, he hadn't even kissed her, only held her close. Other girls would be angry about this, but not Bethany. She didn't want things to move too fast.

"I've seen your mother, you know."

Bethany's blood clotted in her veins, and she was finding it hard to breathe. Her mother died about five years ago in a car accident, an investigative journalist hot on a story, a dedicated woman who never came home. Bethany slowly raised her head. "What do you mean . . . you've seen my mother?"

Sidney shifted uncomfortably. The rain battered against the window.

Stress management, thought Bethany. *Breathe in through the nose, out through the mouth. Purse the lips. Breathe.*

Sidney kissed her. It was long. It was sweet. And Bethany thought her lungs would pop out of her eyeballs. She jerked away, shaking. The muscles around Sidney's eyes contracted, as if he was in pain. "Bad move," he muttered.

"What? The kiss or your comments about my mother?" asked Bethany irritably, sitting up straight and squaring her shoulders.

He didn't reply, but stood up and grabbed his coat. "Gotta go," he said, not looking at her. He left Bethany sitting on the sofa, her arms drawn tightly across her chest as she stared out at the thrashing rain, her insides quivering like the poisonous tentacles of a jellyfish.

Tuesday afternoon

Bethany sat on the bleachers, waiting for Tillie to finish her practice. The cheerleaders ended with a great pyramid extension, then barreled in different directions, pom-poms swishing the air like paper razors.

"Where's Sidney?" asked Tillie, gathering up her gym bag.

"Haven't seen him."

Tillie stood looking at her, one hand resting on her hip. "Problems in lover land? I noticed he didn't sit with us at lunch today."

"I don't want to talk about it," growled Bethany.

"Suit yourself. I'm hungry!"

"You're always hungry. You are nothing but one big stomach."

"Eat your heart out," said Tillie, dragging Bethany through the gym and banging through the double doors.

Charlene Duger pushed past Bethany, her gym bag ramming into Bethany's side. "Hey!" grumbled Bethany. "Take it easy."

"Hey yourself, Witch girl," said Charlene, the words offensive but the tone as smooth as the gym floor. "I hear your boyfriend's going to get creamed!"

"What are you talking about?" asked Tillie, giving Charlene's pixie face the evil eye.

Charlene shrugged and smiled, her blonde corkscrew curls vibrating as if they had an energy all their own. Turning to Bethany, she said, "Isn't Sidney Bluefeather your boyfriend?"

"So what if he is?" asked Bethany.

"I heard he called René Farmore last night. Asked her to some hayride. Her boyfriend is only Judd Reese. You know, star football player, star wrestler? Your little Sidney is toast! But I guess he isn't yours if he's sniffing after René, now, is he?"

"He's not little!" shouted Bethany, her eyes wide at her own vehemence. She resisted the urge to club Charlene over the head with her backpack. René Farmore was one of the beautiful people of the school. Top honors. Farmer's Fair Queen. Nice to teachers, a gorgon to her peers, complete with scalpel-sharp tongue, sinuous body, and bloodthirsty temperament. Just an all-around monstrous, royal pain. If Bethany was to make a list of kids with the killer instinct, René would hold the number one slot. She'd stolen more boyfriends and thrown them away than Ramona had spirits. And Ramona had a lot of spirits, or so she said. "And he's not my boyfriend!" shouted Bethany.

Tillie raised her eyebrows at that one, but didn't comment.

"Whatever," said Charlene, shifting her shoulders and throwing out her hip. "Judd may wait, though, and take him apart at wrestling practice."

"Whoa! Wait," said Tillie. "Wrestling practice? Sidney? I don't think so. Sidney's, well, a geek," she looked hurriedly at Bethany, "I mean, he's not a jock. He's into computers and Native American stuff . . . right?"

Bethany blinked. Sidney? A wrestler? Charlene rustled her pom-poms, her eyes sparkling, realizing, Bethany was sure, that she was the first to dump such spicy news onto Bethany's unsuspecting ears. Charlene shrugged and bounced off, nearly colliding with Janet Atkins.

Bethany and Tillie stared as Janet barked nastily at Charlene, extricating herself from the mass of pom-poms. She wore a long, dark-red velvet dress covered in some sort of black netting. "Get a load of that," whispered Tillie. "She gets worse every day. Too bad Nam already went home. I'd have paid to see that altercation."

"Talking about me?" asked Janet, walking toward them. "I hear the cops were at your house yesterday afternoon and that Alice is dead."

Tillie leaned against the lockers. "Yeah? You seem to hear a lot these days."

"I was sorry to hear about Alice," Bethany said. "I know the two of you were friends."

"Just a second—let me shed a tear of sentiment," moaned Janet in a theatrical voice.

Tillie's brow furrowed. "Are you on drugs or something, girl? Your best friend just got whacked."

"She wasn't my best friend. She wasn't a friend at all. Not that it's any of your business," said Janet.

"Someone certainly didn't like her," said Tillie, "being that she was murdered."

Janet played with the ends of her hair, as if her mind temporarily disconnected from the conversation, then she looked up quickly, smiling. "Did you enjoy your visit with the police?"

Bethany, sensing something strange, kept her voice neutral. "I'm afraid we couldn't help them much. We only met Alice last Saturday. I'm surprised to see you here this afternoon. Someone told me you weren't in classes today."

"I wasn't. I've transferred to Northern. I'm just here to collect the last of my stuff and say goodbye to this disgusting snot-rag of a school. Funny it's you I should run into," she said, staring at Tillie.

René Farmore rounded the corner. "Get a move on, Janet. I've got my car idling out front." She paused and smiled at Bethany. "If it isn't the dynamic Witch duo. Looks like you can't magick your way out of a paper bag, Salem, considering I just bagged your boyfriend."

"You're lying," said Bethany. "Sidney would never go out with you."

René spun on her heels and laughed, grabbing Janet's arm. "Come on! We've got to get going."

Bethany watched them spin down the hall like drunken sailors.

Perhaps she'd just been infected with that emotional flu Cricket talked about the other day, because suddenly she felt so sick she wanted to die. She barely felt Tillie's reassuring hand on her shoulder.

"There were ravens on the stoop this morning," yelled Ramona over the whir of the vacuum cleaner.

Bethany slung her backpack next to her bedroom door and turned around. "And?" Ramona turned, her feet moving in a jaunty sidestep, her white skirt dancing along with the vacuum cleaner. "*And?!*" shouted Bethany.

The housekeeper shut off the machine and sat it upright. "What?"

Bethany extended her nostrils and breathed out like a bull. "The ravens? What about them?"

Ramona swished some cobwebs with a dust cloth. "Things are brewing. The raven offers initiation, protection, and prophecy. They tell of the death of one thing and the birth of another."

"Great."

"How are your studies coming?" asked Ramona, wheeling the vacuum cleaner down the hall.

"I have a lit test tomorrow. Other than that, fine, I guess."

Ramona continued to trundle the cleaner around the corner and out of sight. "Ramona didn't mean your school studies, she meant your occult lessons," came the disembodied voice.

Bethany curled her lip.

The housekeeper reappeared, a feather duster in hand. "Ramona senses something is wrong."

"Don't go there," said Bethany. "I don't want to talk about it."

Ramona nodded her head slowly. "Ah, I see. Trouble in lovers' land?"

Bethany slipped into her bedroom and shut the door. She didn't want to deal with Ramona right now. Sometimes private pain was just that—private. She fluttered her eyes in exasperation as Ramona knocked on the door, then forced herself to open it. "What?"

"Do you know what the word 'gossip' stands for?"

Bethany tilted her head.

"Garbage Of Stupid Silly Ignorant People." With that, Ramona turned on her heel and waltzed down the hall, singing a tune under her breath.

Bethany stood there with a stupefied expression on her face, her eyes flicking up and left then right as if trying to pull a sense of reality from out of her brain, past her brows, and into common sense.

The woman was definitely an enigma.

Witches' Night Out, Bethany's coven, met that night minus Sidney. Gillian was on sabbatical now that she was away at art school, so that left Bethany, Nam, and Tillie. They decided to meet in Bethany's bedroom for more privacy. Hecate sat on the bureau, licking his paws, every now and then checking out his reflection in the mirror as if to say, "My, what a fine specimen I am." Bethany's compact disk player slung out Elven Drums, underpinning the conversation.

"Circle casting," said Nam, resting her Book of Shadows on her knees. The color for this evening was toxic lime green, from the tips of her spike heels to the barrettes in her blue-black hair.

Bethany sighed. "I conjure thee, O circle of power, so that you will be, for me, a boundary between the world of men and the realms of the mighty ones, a meeting place of perfect love, trust, peace, and joy, containing the power I will raise herein. I call upon the east, the south, the west, and the north to aid me in this consecration. In the name of the Lord and the Lady, thus do I conjure thee, O great circle of power!"

Tillie stuffed her face with jellybeans. "Check."

"Quarter calls," said Nam.

"I know them," said Bethany, fingering her pillow.

"Double check," said Tillie, throwing a pink jelly-bean in the air and deftly catching it with her tongue. The beads in her hair snicked back and forth. "Where's Sidney?"

Bethany snorted. "Obviously, he's not here."

"Maybe Judd creamed him," remarked Tillie.

Nam sat back on the bed. "So what's the deal with Sidney? Aren't you two seeing each other anymore?"

"I haven't heard from him," snarled Bethany. "And I don't want to talk about it!"

Nam shook her hand, the lime-green enamel on her fingers glittering in the overhead light. "Put any more edge on your voice and you'll draw blood, honey."

Bethany stuck out her tongue. Hecate amused himself by watching his own tail flick back and forth in the mirror.

Nam closed her eyes, raised her brows, and flattened her lime-green lips. To Bethany, she looked like a tropical fish that went belly-up in the tank. "I hear he's taking René Farmore to the hayride on Wednesday night," said Nam casually.

"Guess that means we're not invited anymore," said Tillie. "What did you do to him, Bethany?"

"Nothing!"

Nam brushed her blue-black hair from her brow. "You didn't tell him we had a meeting tonight, did you?"

Bethany clenched her j----

"No offense," said Tillie. "But that wasn't exactly the right thing to do. I mean, he's still a member of WNO."

"The rule is," said Bethany, feeling the color in her cheeks rising, "one cannot enter the circle angry."

Nam studied the floor. "Is he angry?"

"I'm angry!" yelled Bethany.

Tillie lounged back on the bed. "So, because you're mad, he can't come. Somehow that doesn't exactly seem fair. I thought it was supposed to be the other way around?"

Bethany fumed, jerking the receiver from the phone and waving it at Tillie. "Fine! Call him. I'll leave!"

Nam made tittering noises with her tongue.

"Cat fight!" yelled Tillie, then she grinned. "We don't want you to leave. You're the leader. We can't have a coven if you back out. Tell us what happened the last time you saw him. Maybe we can help." Bethany slammed the receiver back down. "I told you, I don't want to talk about it!"

Tillie made her fingers into claws and snarled at the air. Hecate hissed and clawed back.

"Moon phases," quipped Nam.

"Do we have to do this?" asked Bethany.

Tillie took another handful of jellybeans from the bowl in her lap. "There are eight phases," crunch, "four quarters," crunch. "Each has significance for raising power," crunch-crunch, "and for planning ritual and spell work. Each affects the human mind in its own special way."

"And those ways are?" asked Nam, leering at her.

"Brown nose," said Bethany.

Tillie stuck her finger on her nose. "Indeed it is," she said in awe. "I never noticed."

"I'll take away your jellybeans," threatened Bethany.

Tillie clutched the bowl protectively. "You wouldn't dare! Interesting that Sidney would choose the *femme fatale* of the school. I mean, René has a wake of broken and bleeding hearts. Like, she's been *more* than around."

"She parts the sea of male testosterone," said Nam. "All bow in her wake."

"Not this girl," said Tillie, juggling a few jellybeans in the air.

"I bet she's Attila the Hun reincarnated," said Nam.

Tillie ate another jellybean, holding the bowl tightly, watching Bethany like a hawk. "I bet Sidney is just trying to make you jealous."

Bethany steamed.

"Just so you all know," said Nam. "My moonstone ring is missing."

"You're kidding!" exclaimed Tillie. "That's three pieces of jewelry you've lost in the last few days. What gives?"

The phone rang, jangling Bethany's nerves. She rolled over on her stomach to catch the receiver, dodging a flying jellybean. Hecate leapt off the bureau, snagging the candy and batting it right into Bethany's nose. Tillie sniggered. "Who is it?" Bethany barked into the receiver, rubbing her nose.

Nam made tsking sounds. "The epitome of politeness."

"I want a corn dog," said Tillie.

Bethany shushed her. "Who?"

Cricket stood at the end of the drive, shivering in little more than a flannel nightshirt, her feet bare, the foul November wind licking at the puddle-sodden hem of her gown. She craned her neck, looking for the headlights, hoping that when they appeared, the pinpricks of light would belong to Bethany Salem and not Cricket's father. Her teeth chattered and she hugged herself tightly. Bethany had to come. She just had to! In the distance, she heard the soft sounds of a fiddle. Where was that coming from? In her hand, she clutched another cursed object. She'd found it in the back of the station wagon this evening, tied around one of Tad's old sneakers.

Chapter 12

Nam stared through the windshield of Bethany's car, leaning forward, her hands on the dash. The first bits of a soaking drizzle mixed with flecks of ice started when they left the house. Now the roads were rain slicked and blacker than the jellybeans in Tillie's pocket. Bethany's greatest fear was driving on black ice. Perhaps this wasn't such a good idea. Her hands gripped the steering wheel as she slowly crept down the road. "I think the turnoff is close," said Nam. "Slow down."

"I can't go much slower than ten miles an hour," Bethany said through clenched teeth, but she took her foot off the gas.

"Anyone comes roaring over the hill behind us," said Tillie, looking back, "they're gonna take the behind of your car right to the moon. The fact that it's past curfew and if we get stopped by a cop we're graveyard dust doesn't help any, either."

"There it is!" yelled Nam. "Right there. But . . . she's not standing by the mailbox. I thought you said she'd be by the mailbox?"

Bethany angled the car off the road, as close to the box as possible.

"Maybe she went in when it started to rain?" offered Tillie.

"If anyone catches us here, we are more than burnt offerings," complained Nam, looking around fearfully. "Maybe you ought to just pull forward, turn around further down, then head back home. This mush could turn into ice in less than five minutes if the temperature drops. My sister totaled her car last year on 583 because of black ice."

Bethany left the lights on and the motor running. "We came this far, we might as well check it out. You wait here, I'll get out and look."

Bethany stood outside the car, barely able to see, the sound of the windshield wipers on the car snicking methodically. Something long and tangled clung to the branches of a bush by the mailbox. She would have missed it if she hadn't slipped and grabbed onto the bush. With cold fingers she pulled it free and hurried back to the warm interior of the car, soaking wet and scared. She slammed the door, shivering.

"What's the matter?" asked Tillie, leaning over the car seat to get a better look.

Bethany, her heart pounding, held out a torn piece of flannel.

"Eeuuw . . . icky. What's that?" asked Nam, squinting in the dim glow of the dashboard.

Tillie turned on the overhead light. The three girls stared at Bethany's shaking hand. The cloth looked like the ruffle from the bottom of a nightgown. It was sodden, muddy, and laced with blood. "I found this caught on a bush beside the mailbox," said Bethany.

"Are you thinking what I'm thinking?" whispered Tillie.

The girls turned their heads, peering out the rain-splattered windows, but the only movement in sight were the bony fingers of the black bushes by the car door and the glittering, needlelike drops of sleet fizzing in the halo of the headlights. Not a single light shone in any of the buildings on the Bindart farm.

"What do we do?" asked Nam, her voice tiny and fearful, her eyes wide.

"We get the flashlight out of the trunk," said Bethany, "and we take a look around."

"But that's trespassing and I'm wearing spikes!" wailed Nam.

Tillie slapped her lightly on the back of the head. "Your fashion statement is going to get us all killed someday."

"Getting out of the car might get us killed," grumbled Nam.

Bethany opened the car door. "Tillie and I will check it out. You can stay here. If anyone comes by, tell them we stopped to look at the tire. We thought we had a flat."

"How do I explain," said Nam, "that you are checking the tire if you aren't here?"

"You're the smart one," said Tillie. "Think of something."

The two girls slid out of the car and retrieved the flashlight.

Bethany played the light along the ground but enough rain had fallen to wash anything away—like blood. There were gouge marks in the mud beside the mailbox, but they could have been here awhile. She skipped the light along the drive. Nothing but water, ice, sticks, shale, mud, and leaves.

Slowly, they crept up the drive, but found nothing.

"If we go any further," said Tillie, slipping precariously in a rut, "someone is sure to see the flashlight, and we can't go on without it."

Bethany nodded, the frigid rain streaming down her face. She could hardly see. "What do you think we should do?"

Tillie shrugged. "Go back to your house. Dry out. Think. Maybe she just went inside."

"This feels wrong," said Bethany. She was shivering so badly that her stiff lips felt like they were coated in styling gel.

"Sure does."

"What if—"

"Don't think about it," said Tillie. "You haven't gotten one of your visions, have you?"

Bethany's muscles tensed and writhed under her skimpy coat. "No, but that doesn't mean anything. I didn't have any visions about Alice, and she's in the Cedar Crest Funeral Home right about now. In fact, my visions, as you call them, appear to have abandoned me lately." Bethany's arms were so cold she felt like they would contract into nothing. "Maybe I'm not going to get the visions anymore. Maybe it was all just a fluke. Maybe I just made it all up in my head."

"Maybe you're lovesick and nothing can get through."

Bethany grimaced. "A pleasant thought."

Tillie stepped in a puddle and lifted her soaked sneaker with a grimace. "But not particularly helpful at the moment."

They slogged back to the car. Nam was not there. The gentle, rapid ding signaling the open door was lost in the torrential downpour. The girls cast frightened eyes at each other, then Bethany played the light along the ground, following spike holes in the mud from Nam's shoes. Around the mailbox. A yard or two down the driveway, then off into the bushes.

"Aw, rats," muttered Tillie.

"Nam?" called Bethany, trying to keep her voice down, but needing to yell over the pounding rain. So much for the drizzle.

No answer.

"Darn it, Nam!" shouted Tillie. "Where are you?"

"Over here!" came a small voice.

Tillie and Bethany slogged forward as best they could, battering through broken branches, thigh-high weeds, and double the mud.

"Here!"

Bethany shot the light ahead, illuminating Nam standing defiantly over a crumpled form, her lime-green stretch pants melded to shivering, slender legs, a tire iron raised in her hand as if she was about to do battle with the deadliest of phantoms. "Here! She's right here!" Nam pointed with the tire iron. "Something's wrong with her."

"You didn't hit her, did you?" asked Tillie.

"Oh, please," said Nam, lowering the tire iron. "As if I could strike an innocent person. I was only ready because I thought you were somebody else. You should have told me to bring my baseball bat."

"Who? Did you see someone?" asked Bethany, a little out of breath.

"I saw a shadow, but it booked when you two started crashing through the woods."

Tillie gently rolled the body over. "It's Cricket."

"Is she still breathing?" asked Bethany.

"Yep, but we better get her out of this rain."

"Maybe we shouldn't move her," said Nam, stooping over the inert girl. "We don't know what's wrong with her."

"We can't leave her out here," said Tillie. "Bethany, bring the light closer." Tillie stooped down, carefully checking Cricket. "Looks like a nasty bump on her head," she pointed at the raised skin, but it was hard to see in such minimal light and the blinding rain. "One of us is going to have to go to the house for help."

Bethany groaned. No one wanted to face Old Man Bindart, especially her.

"I can't go," said Nam. "I almost broke my neck just getting over here." She raised a mud-slicked, spiked foot. "As it is, these heels are ruined! And they went so well with my stretch pants!"

"Looked at those pants recently? You've got a big tear right below the knee. You ever heard the words 'trailer-trash'?" asked Tillie. "Next thing you'll be wearing leopard pants, and then you can just go prowl around another coven!"

Nam half-heartedly swung the tire iron at her.

Tillie ducked, giggling. "Got to get up earlier in the morning to get me with that thing." She sighed. "I'll go." Tillie took off her coat and laid it over Cricket. "You guys stay here. Maybe Bethany can stoke up her healing engine."

The two girls watched Tillie stumble toward the driveway. Bethany knelt over Cricket, but she was shaking so badly she couldn't concentrate.

"What if whoever did this to Cricket is still out there?" asked Nam fearfully.

Bethany looked up, then over to Tillie's retreating back. What should she do? If she left Nam alone, she'd be in danger. If she stayed here, Tillie might not make it to the house. Cricket was breathing and her pulse seemed okay. She was just out cold. "When help comes, stick the tire iron in your pants. We don't want anyone to think you hit her."

"In my pants!? Talk about a pole up your—hey! You're not going to leave me here alone, are you?"

"Start screaming 'fire'," said Bethany. "And don't stop."

"What? Out here? In this godforsaken place? In this rain?"

"Just do it!"

Nam began yelling and Bethany chased after Tillie, screaming the word 'fire'. Tillie turned, paused, then caught on, joining the chorus. Bethany stood at the end of the drive, between the two, screaming her lungs out, her head coated in icy rain, spikes of her long hair stiffly whipping through the air as she turned her head back and forth to hear both girls. The great thing about the country, she thought wildly, is that you could have a beer party and the entire valley echoes with the laughter and music. She guessed that three screaming teens could do the same amount of sound damage, even in the pounding rain.

Lights started to flick on, including a flood by the mailbox. She didn't stop yelling until Tillie emerged from the gloom, several figures trailing behind her.

"Why is it," said Old Man Bindart, "that every time there's serious trouble around here lately, I find you somewhere around it?"

Bethany stared at the cracked linoleum floor of the drafty Bindart kitchen, trying to ignore the gloom of the yellowed walls and ancient, chipped porcelain sink. *That refrigerator must be thirty years old,* she thought. *And a wood stove? For cooking?* She glanced at Tillie and Nam, who appeared to be as miserable as she felt. Poor Nam looked like a diseased worm coated in green slime, water dripping off her nose, her makeup trailing down her pale cheeks like bad Goth, standing ramrod straight, a distressed expression clearly showing on her face.

Bethany saw the bulge of the tire iron in Nam's pants and stepped quickly in front of her.

"You wanna explain what you were doing on my property in the first place?" Old Man Bindart asked, his big arms crossed in front of his barrel chest. Mrs. Bindart floated around behind him, not uttering a sound. She looked like a worn-out version of Cricket.

Bethany glanced at the kitchen curtains. A hundred years old. At least there were only a few cobwebs.

"Well?"

The girls remained mute.

Mrs. Bindart set a tray of mugs on the table, steaming with hot cocoa. "Shut up, Jim."

He stared at her, his eyes round with disbelief. All three girls leaned toward Mrs. Bindart, as if examining a new species of bug.

Mrs. Bindart cleared her throat and wiped her hands on an apron so faded that the print, whatever it had been, was barely visible. "I said, shut up, and I meant just that!" She stared at him defiantly. "They've done us a good turn. Take it for what it is."

Old Man Bindart stuttered, but nothing came out.

"There will be plenty of time for explanations later," she said, her voice growing stronger, her small shoulders squaring. "Right now, we have one daughter gone, one with a concussion and possible head trauma, and a son in the hospital. We're three for three. I suggest you get your head out of your behind." She turned to Nam. "Look at you shivering. Would you like to sit down, dear?"

Nam threw a hateful look at Bethany. "No, thank you, ma'am."

And then, to their collective amazement, Old Man Bindart began to cry—huge, rasping sounds that cut to the soul.

Chapter 13

Tuesday morning

Tuesday morning left a light blanket of snow as an early winter present for the residents of Cedar Crest. Bethany picked up Nam and Tillie, as neither had enough money for snow treads on their cars. "Enjoy it now, ladies," said Bethany as they rode to school. "If I don't make my car payment, the Camaro is history."

"That's awful!" exclaimed Nam. Today was a red day. Her glossy blood-red lips were exceptionally fetching. Bethany thought that Nam looked like she'd just snacked on a human neck or two. Ugh. Tillie passed a box of tissues around in the car and they all blew their noses.

"It's gonna look weird that we're all fighting off colds at the same time," said Tillie, grabbing for another tissue.

"We can't very well explain we were rescuing a damsel in distress," said Nam, as Bethany pulled into the school parking lot and headed for her numbered slot. "Everybody already thinks we're strange."

"Hey! Somebody's in your spot!" said Tillie.

"Oh, man," whispered Nam, "it's René's car. See the vanity plate?"

Bethany gripped the steering wheel. Too bad her hockey stick was in her room rather than in the back of her car. More disconcerting, a raven was perched as big as you please on top of René's silver BMW. "I hope that bird craps on her car!" muttered Bethany. She lowered her window. "Hey! Bird! Do me a favor. Go to the potty on that car!" The raven regarded her silently and turned his back while Nam giggled and squealed.

"Nice try," said Tillie.

Bethany turned to her friends. "Listen, I'll drop you guys off at the front door, then circle around and see if I can find a spot in the back lot."

Naturally, she was late for Economics and Mr. Pratt was none too kind as she tried to slither into her seat. "That will be one infraction, Miss Salem," he said, handing her a yellow slip of paper. "That's three in one month."

René, sitting at the front of the room, made a loud guffaw when Mr. Pratt announced that Bethany could kindly take part in one of the school's finest services—detention.

Bethany seethed.

A flash of red bolted down the hall, clunky crimson heels skittering into Bethany. Nam's shoulders were shaking, the red ball earrings in her lobes bouncing like crazed ladybugs. "What did you do?" she squealed at Bethany.

Bethany looked at Nam with something less than irritation. "What are you talking about?"

"René's car," twittered Nam. "You know, her car?"

"Look, Nam, I don't have time for this. Thanks to that snot, I have detention, and if I don't move it, I could be in worse trouble!"

"You mean you *really* don't know?" panted Nam.

Bethany hurried down the hall, Nam awkwardly trailing after her as best she could on her new shoes. "Tell me," said Bethany, "if you tap the heels of those stupid shoes together, will you go home and leave me alone?"

"Some day I'll conjure a house to fall on you!" snapped Nam. "You know, I hope you have an alibi for the last two hours!"

Bethany, exasperated, stopped, turning slowly. Nam pitched forward and almost brought them both down. "What," asked Bethany, "are you talking about?"

Nam stared at Bethany, then grabbed her arm and teetered in the opposite direction, saying, "Out of my way. Out of my way, people," as she dragged Bethany along to the front door.

"I can't see anything," said Bethany, peering outside. "There's just a lot of sunshine and melting snow."

Other students were also gathered at the front doors—some laughing, some making horrible faces.

"Look again!" said Nam, pushing Bethany's nose closer to the window.

"What's all that white stuff on René's car?" asked Bethany. "Did it snow again?"

"Bird doo-doo," whispered Nam, a twinkle in her green eyes.

"No!"

"Oh-h-h yeah," said Nam. "And I specifically heard you tell that raven sitting on her car to crap all over it!" she said loudly.

"Shut up, Nam. I did no such thing! At least, not on purpose. I mean, I didn't really think . . . " But it was too late. A few of the other students stepped away from Bethany, staring at Nam. "Hey, that girl just said she put a spell on René's car!" shouted one kid. "Teach me to do that!"

Bethany groaned. "Nam, you are *so* dead."

"Where have you been?" asked Tillie, zipping her gym bag, fumbling as she sneezed. "Practice was over twenty minutes ago. I thought you left without me." They stood in the hall, outside the gym.

Bethany sighed. "Double detention, then a visit to the guidance office to explain that I did not threaten René Farmore with magick."

"You're kidding!"

Bethany could hear a succession of whistle blows and pounding feet from the interior of the gym. "What's going on in there?" she asked, looking at the closed doors.

"Wrestling practice starts today. They'll make their cuts the first week in December."

Bethany stared at the doors. "Sidney in there?"

Tillie looked at her sideways. "Guess so. René's dad is the coach, you know. Right now, she's screaming up a storm about her car. I got to say, you did a major job on her."

Bethany's voice carried the annoyance she felt. "I did not do anything to her car!"

"Yeah, sure," said Tillie. "And Witches melt when you throw water on them."

The gym doors flew open and René stalked out, her face red, eyes wild, blonde hair streaming behind her. She stopped dead when she saw Bethany. "I'll get you, you Witch! People like you should be locked up! Everybody laughs at you, you know. You and your freak friends! And I'll have you know, Sidney is very, very good . . . if you understand my drift." She wiggled a slender hip. "By the time I get done with him, he'll be nothing but a piece of heartbroken Indian refuse!" She turned on her heel and stormed down the hall.

Bethany rocked on the balls of her feet, ready to run down the hall and tackle the little snotball, but Tillie grabbed her arm with a grip like Godzilla. "Not here. Not now," whispered Tillie. "There's always a time and a place."

Bethany followed her glumly out of the building and into the parking lot. "Maybe we could conjure up some nasty gnomes to carry her away into the bowels of the earth," seethed Bethany.

"With your track record, I wouldn't even think about that if I were you," said Tillie. "She'll get hers. They always do. Where's Nam?" asked Tillie, throwing her bag in the car.

"Ducking me. I can't believe she got me into so much hot water. She literally bellowed to everyone about that bird crap thing. I have no idea what got into her head. I think she needs another lesson on the Witches' Pyramid—To Know, To Dare, To Will, and To Be SILENT. Actually, she got a job at the flower shop on Market Street," said Bethany. "One of her sisters picked her up after school because I had detention." Bethany stowed her backpack in the trunk of the car.

"She ought to blend right in with all those exotic flowers," said Tillie, adjusting the front seat. "So now what?" She sneezed, digging a tissue out of her purse.

"Hand me one of those, will you? We're going to visit Cricket Bindart."

"What?" Sneeze. "No!" Double sneeze. "Why?" asked Tillie, handing over the tissue and blowing her own nose at the same time.

"Because she wanted to see us last night, and I think someone attacked her," said Bethany, starting up the car. "Let's face it. She didn't just go wandering in the woods in her nightgown in the freezing rain."

"We don't know that," said Tillie. "Maybe she just fell."

"Yeah, right, she fell and then dragged herself off the driveway, away from the house."

"So maybe she lost her sense of direction." Sneeze. "Besides, you know they aren't going to let us see her."

Bethany swung purposefully around to the front parking lot, drifting past René's bird dropping-encrusted car. "I'll be . . . " she whispered. "Oh man, and the window was open!"

"Told you. That will certainly gag her," said Tillie. "You better start watching what you wish for."

Bethany's mind drifted. "Yeah," she whispered. "Yeah."

"Let's stop at the florist and pick up some flowers for Cricket," said Tillie. "I've got a couple of bucks in my wallet and maybe Nam can give us a discount. Do you have any money?"

"I think I have a few dollars."

Mrs. Bindart did not look like the same woman. This person answered the door with her hair done in a neat braid, a nice blue dress, makeup, and a new apron. This woman smiled. She had those same mystical blue eyes like the twins. They reminded Bethany of the sea. "And you brought flowers!" she gushed. "Go right on up," she said, motioning toward the stairs. "Cricket's room is in the attic. Please don't make no nevermind to the housekeeping. I sort of let it go these past two years, but I'm in the process of changing that now."

The girls stepped over several gallons of white paint and assorted house decorating and cleaning paraphernalia. Tillie sneezed. Bethany did the same. "Boy, aren't we a pair."

Cricket was in her bed, dwarfed by multiple faded comforters and several pillows. Her face looked pinched and pale, her eyes closed. A dusting of blue danced across her cheeks.

"She looks awful," whispered Tillie, "maybe we'd better go . . . "

Cricket slowly opened her eyes. "Bethany," she whispered through cracked lips.

"You look lousy," said Tillie.

Bethany elbowed Tillie in the ribs and gave her a dirty look. "We just thought we'd stop by and see if we could get you anything," said Bethany. She held out a bouquet of flowers. "Nam sent these along." She didn't want to admit that neither she nor Tillie could scrounge up enough to pay for the flowers.

Cricket tried to reach for the flowers but fell back, exhausted, on the pillow.

"I'll just put them on your dresser," said Bethany, setting the flowers in front of the mirror and unwrapping the green tissue around the blooms. "Do you feel like talking?"

Cricket nodded her head.

Tillie stepped forward. "What happened to you last night?"

Cricket coughed and winced, running a limp hand through her oily copper hair. "I called you guys because I think someone at the farm poisoned Alice. I wanted to talk to you about it, but while I was waiting for you by the mailbox, someone jumped me from behind. I don't remember anything past that. My mother tells me . . ." she paused and smiled. "Mom talking. I can hardly believe it! Anyway, my parents said that you guys found me and raised the alarm. I can't thank you enough."

"It was no big deal," said Tillie. "Why do you think someone here poisoned Alice?"

Cricket ran a pale hand over the comforter. "The police said that the poison was in an apple. I gave Alice an apple the Sunday she died. I think it was the same one."

"Did you tell the police?" asked Bethany.

Cricket shook her head, sucking pensively on her lower lip. "No. I didn't want them to think I did it."

"Where did you get the apple?" asked Tillie.

Cricket's eyes filled with tears. "From Clarence."

"I don't know Clarence very well," said Bethany hurriedly, "but I don't think he would ever intentionally harm anyone, especially you."

Cricket's lower lip trembled. "Maybe not, but he's the one who gave it to me."

Tillie moved restlessly around the room. "What do you want us to do about it?" she asked. "We're sort of on the outside looking in."

Cricket clutched the comforter with desperate fingers. "Look, someone wants the Bindart farm to close down. If it does, my family will have nowhere to go. The bank loan's overextended. This morning I heard my father saying that someone broke into the grading shed and ruined the cider machine and sliced the conveyor belts to ribbons. He says it will cost over a thousand dollars to fix the damage. It's got to stop! Maybe if you came back here to work, people will be afraid of you and it will stop?"

"As in our reputation precedes us?" Tillie laughed. "I don't think that will help. Not too many people are afraid of a couple of sixteen-year-olds." Tillie turned away, looking at Bethany out of the corner of her eye.

"Nam already got a new job working at the flower shop in town," said Bethany.

"Thanksgiving vacation starts for us on Thursday," said Tillie. "We'll have a total of five days off. Maybe we could snoop around."

Bethany smiled, trying not to sound too harsh. "This is something Tillie and I have to talk about, if it's okay with you."

Cricket sobbed. "You're right. It's too much to ask." She put her hands over her mouth and silently stared at the ceiling.

Tillie dipped her head, the beads in her hair rustling quietly in the claustrophobic little room.

"Why don't your parents just call the police?" asked Bethany.

"I don't know!" wailed Cricket. "Maybe because they are too proud, maybe because they can't face the truth, or maybe because one of my family members is behind it all! Then, there's Leslee." Her voice died in her throat. "She's, um, not around at the moment. And now someone is dead!"

Bethany chewed on her lip. "Did Leslee go on another business trip?"

"Not exactly."

Cricket remained silent. It was obvious she wasn't going to say anything more about Leslee. *Odd*, thought Bethany, *but you can't expect people to tell you everything.* She switched her line of questioning. "Did anyone hear you call me last night?"

Cricket shook her head listlessly.

"Or see you walk out to the mailbox?"

"No. No one that I'm aware of. Though right before someone jumped me, I did hear a fiddle playing." She laughed, then coughed. "But that certainly doesn't have anything to do with anything."

Bethany stepped over to the flowers, arranging them a bit, feeling the soft petals between her fingers. Roses, baby's breath, carnations . . . "Where is your brother?" she asked.

"He's still in the hospital," said Cricket, fear touching her voice. "Something about infection, but my parents won't say more than that."

Tillie picked up a book off Cricket's worn and battered desk. "Shakespeare?"

Cricket smiled. "Even home-schooled kids have to study," she said.

Tillie stepped backward and knocked a math book off the desk. She stooped to pick it up. "Hello? What's this?" she asked, pulling at something stuck beneath the desk. A long strip of rawhide emerged, entangled with several red feathers. The entire mess was coated in dust. "A bookmark?"

Cricket struggled to sit up straight. "Now I remember! I had one of those in my hand last night. Except it was a newer one. I found it in the station wagon Tad and I share, but it must have gotten lost outside. I've never seen that one before, but it looks just like the one I found. Those are feathers from a rooster." She coughed again.

"Do you have chickens on the farm?" asked Tillie. "I don't remember seeing any."

"We used to," said Cricket, "but when mother took ill, they all died off. We still have the hen house, though."

"Was this always your room?" asked Bethany.

Cricket shook her head. "No, it was Tad's but he moved to the migrant worker's house over the summer, so he said I could have it. My bedroom was on the second floor with all the others before that."

"Mind if we take this?" asked Tillie.

Cricket's eyelids fluttered. "I don't care. Take it."

Tillie threw the object over to Bethany. "You can carry it," she said.

"Oh, you're too kind," answered Bethany, catching the feathered mess in her hand. "Cricket? There's one more thing. You wouldn't happen to know what kind of rabbit you found in the mailbox, would you?"

Cricket closed her eyes and opened them again. "Tad said that he thinks they were some rare kind." She paused. "Chinchilla, I think he said. He tried to find out where they came from. He was going to ask the ag teacher at your school if he knew anyone that had them."

Tillie stared at Cricket. "Why would he ask at our school?"

"Clarence makes feed and produce deliveries there every week. Sometimes Tad rides along. I think he shouldn't because he gets so upset when he sees the school. We used to have so much fun together at home, but when Dad said he couldn't have a computer last year, his whole attitude changed. Now, he really hates being here. Anyway, he knows the teacher and some of the kids. He was going to ask around but then he got hurt and never had the chance."

Tillie contemplated this for a moment. "You know, Cricket, I bet if you guys had a chance to choose and had a little more freedom to socialize, you might just think you have the better deal. If it wouldn't be for the extracurricular activities, I think I might do home-schooling, too. I can understand how the desire for a computer changed his attitude."

"You're kidding!"

"No," said Tillie solemnly. "I'm not."

"What's with you and this home-schooling jag?" asked Bethany. "What, your friends aren't good enough for you?"

"It's not that," said Tillie. "I read a study by a college professor last year that really got me to thinking. He said that today's teens aren't like the kids in the fifties. He claims that we are more mature and that we shouldn't be in high school at all. He feels that we should go on to college at fifteen or enter a trade school. I've been thinking a lot about that article and Cricket's situation. I think that professor guy is right, but so many kids can't afford college, which means they'd be out on the streets at fifteen. It's like the educational system has us in a holding pattern because they can't figure out what to do with us."

"I have to admit, Tillie, some of what you're saying seems right, but then we'd have to give up the sports, club activities, and the prom. Somehow that doesn't seem fair."

Tillie stood in the Bindart driveway, looking glumly at the sky. "I guess there's no easy solution."

Bethany laughed. "Not to our educational system and not to that stupid Witch's ladder," said Bethany. "Ramona was telling me about them. Black feathers are definitely a curse, unless you are trying to banish something, but I don't know what red ones are for."

Tillie shivered, fumbling with the car door.

"Why are you wearing a windbreaker? Where's your winter coat?" asked Bethany.

"I didn't want my mother to see my dirty coat, so I shoved it under my bed. This is the only other jacket I had."

"Where's your wool cheerleading jacket?"

"At the cleaners. My mother thought it would be nice and shipped it off last week. I should have it back tomorrow," said Tillie through chattering teeth. She hopped in the car. "Just get this thing started, will you? I would bet money that those rabbits the Bindart twins found were the same ones taken from our school, which means the Bindarts have something in common with someone who goes to our school."

Bethany nodded. "Agreed. So who do we know that they have in common?"

"Janet," they chorused in unison.

"I don't know," replied Tillie. "This all seems a little off the wall, even for Janet."

"Okay. How about Janet's mythical boyfriend? Maybe he found out Tad was messing around with Janet and decided to take revenge?"

"By destroying the whole family? It's possible. Someone sure doesn't like them. What are we going to do?" asked Tillie, opening a new package of tissues and blowing her nose, handing one to Bethany at the same time.

Bethany turned the key in the ignition and backed out of the Bindart driveway. "Someone's definitely trying to mess with that family. Maybe Tad's doing all this. That was his room and Cricket said she found the Witch's ladder in his car. He does visit the school with Clarence, Cricket said so."

Tillie shook her head, the beads in her hair clacking. "He's in the hospital. He can't make a new Witch's ladder without someone asking him what he's doing, besides he can't be at the hospital and the farm at the same time. For all we know, he could be knocked out cold from all the drugs they're giving him."

"Someone could be helping him," replied Bethany.

"No. It doesn't fit when you take into account the sabotage of the property. Why would Tad want to ruin his father's business?"

"Maybe to get out of there. He might think that if the family business goes under, they will have to move and his father can't act like some crazed potentate."

Tillie drummed her fingers on the dashboard. "It's possible, but it doesn't feel right. It could be like you said the other day—that there's more than one mystery here, and they appear to have intertwined at the same time."

"Intertwined?"

Tillie narrowed her eyes. "I've been studying for the SATs. My mother bought flashcards. I can also tell you what the word 'ameliorate' means."

"Lucky me."

"Aren't you going to ask me what it means?"

Bethany sighed and pulled out onto Old Mill Road. "Do tell."

"It means 'to make better, improve, or relieve.' We're going to ameliorate Cricket's predicament."

"We are?" asked Bethany, as she turned left onto Baltimore Street.

"Absolutely," replied Tillie.

"Why do I feel I'm losing my leadership capabilities?" asked Bethany, running her fingers over the steering wheel while they waited for a light to change.

"You want to help her as much as I do," said Tillie. "Besides, you can't keep your nose out of a mystery even if you tried."

Bethany refused to answer as she turned left onto Simpson Alley and slowed for another red light.

"I also know what an equilateral triangle is."

"And I'm sure you're going to enlighten me." While they waited for the light to change, Bethany withdrew the rawhide from her pocket, dangling it in the air. "None of this makes any real sense. I really think we've overlooked something. We don't know any of these people very well. Northern County isn't our usual stomping grounds. I feel like I'm in a dark tunnel without the slightest possibility of illumination."

"We could go back to work there."

"Oh, happy day, but you heard what Cricket said. Leslee isn't around and she's the one that offered us our jobs back. With her gone, Old Man Bindart may not hire us, but if you want me to I'll call this afternoon." The light turned green and Bethany accelerated.

"Watch out!" screamed Tillie. A black Bronco rocketed through the intersection and smashed into the front side panel of Bethany's car. Both air bags exploded. By the time they'd disentangled themselves, the Bronco was long gone. Bethany stood shivering in the cold, brushing the chemical dust from the airbag off her coat. Her beautiful Camaro looked like a bent, blood-red twist-tie.

Tillie leaned on the car, looking over at Bethany. "This wreck is definitely not an equilateral triangle."

Bethany stared at what was left of her car, her eyes filling with tears.

"Look at the bright side," said Tillie. "No more car payments."

"My father is going to kill me," moaned Bethany.

Chapter 14

Tuesday evening

Ramona is going out this evening," said the housekeeper, bustling around the kitchen, her white skirt flapping about her legs. Bethany wondered first, if Ramona ever got tired of white, and second, how the heck she always kept her clothing so clean. Must be a Hoodoo secret. Hecate jumped at the hem of Ramona's skirt, then flew back as she shushed him away. "Silly old cat." She turned to Bethany. "There's a meatloaf in the oven. Help yourself. Ramona is sorry about your pretty car, but you couldn't keep up the payments anyway. It's a good thing your father insisted on gap insurance. You won't get anything back, but you won't owe anything but the deductible. Spirit just decided to move that car out of your life for you."

Bethany looked at her sourly. "Yeah, and raise my insurance rates in the process. How kind."

"It will be okay," said Ramona, stopping to pat Bethany on the shoulder. "We must thank Spirit that neither you nor Tillie were injured. I will burn a candle tonight."

Bethany crossed her arms tightly across her chest, squeezing herself to keep from screaming. After all, it wasn't Ramona's fault Bethany lost her car.

Ramona paused. "You didn't do anything to someone, did you?"

"What do you mean?"

Ramona's dark eyes regarded her with a critical squint. "Magickally. You didn't attack anyone? Because you know if you did, then you are experiencing the rule of three. May I remind you that what you give out comes back to you three times, or once in a very big way. To defend is a fine thing—to attack, quite another. And then there's the level of attack. You can defend, but you cannot use more force than necessary. But you know that. Ethics are such a difficult subject. I'm sure you are aware of the dangers."

Bethany's heart fluttered as she thought of the bird poop on René's car. She swallowed uneasily.

The doorbell rang. Ramona beamed. "Oh! Ramona must go!"

Bethany looked up. "You cast a love spell on Officer Charles, didn't you?" she queried, hoping to get back at the Creole wisdom now picking at her conscience.

Ramona, eyes wide, turned to face Bethany. "*Moi?* Me? No! Those love spells can get you into a lot of trouble, *ma cherie*. Better to ask the universe to bring you the energy of love instead—you dare not target a specific person. True, sometimes Spirit will bring you a friend, even a pet, though you may have thought you wanted passion." She chortled. "Believe me, I've seen too many love spells gone bad."

"He ate your cookies. I know you magick the food," Bethany insisted, not willing to let the topic go.

Ramona grinned. "I cannot help it if my cooking carries a magick of its own! For peace, for harmony, for healing . . . oh, yes . . . Ramona's dishes carry much enchantment!"

"Where's Ramona?" asked Tillie, throwing her wool cheerleading coat in the hallway chair.

"I see you got your coat back."

"Lucky me, it was in the hall when I got home. My parents were ballistic about the accident. They didn't want me to drive over here this evening. My father says you're the seventh teen he knows of this month that cracked up their car. He was ready to pull my keys but my mother doesn't want her Durango to turn into a bus, so she won the argument. She's already been complaining that she doesn't have any time for herself because she's running my little brother all over the place. Between play practice, band, and the youth church group, she barely has enough time to think. We've been eating a lot of microwave meals lately. This, I believe, is why my father succumbed."

"Succumbed?"

"SATs."

"Right."

The ticking of the grandfather clock beside the chair bounced off the walls, driving Bethany crazy. Someday she was going to accidentally break that stupid clock. "To answer your earlier question, Ramona is out with Officer Charles," said Bethany. "I think he has a thing for her."

"For Ramona? Wow!"

Nam arrived a few minutes later, drifting into the family room. "I phoned Sidney," she said, her tone daring Bethany to say anything. "He should be a part of this, too."

"Oh, great," said Bethany, flopping down on the sofa.

"You're going to have to talk to him sometime," said Nam. "You might as well get it over with."

"With you two as an audience? I don't think so," said Bethany.

Tillie pulled a candy bar out of her purse. Hecate pounded in her lap, his whiskers quivering. Tillie pushed him aside. "Mine," she said. "All mine! Cats don't like chocolate!"

"Tell that to Hecate," said Bethany. "He thinks he's a person."

Tillie took a bite, chewed, then shook the end of the candy bar at Bethany. "You've got to put your differences aside until we figure this mess out, okay? Someone purposefully hit your car today and fled the scene. We could have been killed."

Bethany stubbornly said nothing.

When Sidney knocked on the front door it was Tillie who let him in. He refused to look Bethany in the eye and sat at the other end of the sofa, placing his backpack between them as an extra protective barrier. It was all Bethany could do to keep from going insane.

"First," said Tillie, assuming leadership, "we have to de-magick this stupid thing." She threw the Witch's ladder on the coffee table. Nam visibly recoiled. "Then we have to figure out what the heck is going on. The first part is easy. The second is a dilly." She looked over at Sidney. "Did you bring what I asked you?"

He reached in his backpack and pulled out an unopened bottle of vinegar. "Violà!" he said, setting the vinegar on the coffee table with a flourish.

Nam picked at a fingernail. "Okay, what do we have? And what facts do we keep, and what do we throw away?"

Bethany was so upset, she couldn't think. She didn't know which was worse, not having her car, not having Sidney, or slowly losing her leadership over the group. She didn't realize, until now, how much she liked Sidney, and how angry she was that he was going out with René. And why hadn't Judd creamed him yet? She cracked her knuckles. Nam looked at her curiously.

Tillie broke the uncomfortable silence. "Maybe we should write down everything we know, and then take it from there? In the meantime, Bethany, why don't you go get your cauldron and we'll get rid of that Witch's ladder thing."

Bethany stomped out of the family room in search of her cauldron. Nowhere in the house. She slid into her coat, pausing at the back door, hearing laughter floating through the house from the family room. Sidney said something and the girls twittered. Anger flashed through Bethany as she threw open the door. She found the cauldron on the patio, filled with debris and water. The sun was spitting the last of its fiery plumage across the sky. It took her several minutes to clean out the cauldron, her frustration mounting until she sat back on her haunches and began to cry. Some good leader she was! Cricket's family was in trouble, Alice was dead, her car was totaled, and all she could think about was a dumb boy. To top it off, she was afraid to wish anything for fear it would come true! How could you have feelings and still be a Witch? This whole occult thing was harder than she ever thought possible! And now Tillie was naturally taking over the group, only because Bethany didn't have her head screwed on right. She gripped the edges of the metal cauldron until her knuckles turned white. They were all in there, doing the right thing, having fun, and she was out here, hating everyone and everything. She despised herself most of all. Why did people have to be born with feelings, anyway? Bethany wiped the tears from her eyes, sure that she'd messed up her makeup. She couldn't walk back in there looking like a crybaby.

A raven circled overhead in the gathering dusk, then landed at the edge of the patio. It stood there, cawing softly, head cocked, a large, glittering eye staring her down.

Bethany blinked away the tears. "You are definitely creeping me out," she whispered to the bird. "And you got me into trouble." He ruffled his feathers, but didn't answer. "I don't know what your name is," she said softly. "And I don't understand why you are here, but if you could in any way help me—"

A streak of black burst from the open kitchen door, flying across the patio. Hecate! "No!" shouted Bethany, jumping to her feet and dropping the cauldron. The cat lunged at the raven while the cauldron clanged on the flagstone of the patio. "Hecate! Stop!" yelled Bethany, lurching awkwardly toward the cat and catching only a few tail hairs in her fingers.

The raven took flight, barely escaping the snapping jaws of the feline. The bird continued to rise in the air, screaming. Bethany was sure if she could understand bird language there might be some swear words in there. "Hecate!" she said angrily. The cat turned, his ears flattened, his pointy teeth wet with kitty saliva. "Shame on you!" Hecate stuck his tail in the air and marched back into the house, never once uttering an apology. Territory was, after all, territory.

Bethany retrieved the cauldron and stared at the gathering gloom. Not a star or a feather to be seen.

Someone turned on a light in the kitchen and a golden beam picked out something metal in the dying grass at the edge of the patio. Wasn't that where the bird landed? She set the cauldron down and moved forward slowly. She held the object under the beam of kitchen light. A key. The old-fashioned kind. Like one of those skeleton keys used in houses near the turn of the last century. Her grandmother used to keep a set of these on a key ring by the kitchen door when she was a little girl. She hefted the key in her hand. Solid. Heavy.

"Bethany!"

She whirled, putting the key in her pocket.

Sidney stepped out onto the patio. "Are you all right? I heard something fall."

Bethany turned away, not wanting him to see her tear-swollen eyes. "I'm fine. Go back inside. I found the cauldron. I had to clean it out. Dropped it, I guess."

He moved forward and she backed away, averting her face from the kitchen light, allowing the shadows to cool her hot cheeks.

"Listen," he said. "I'm sorry about the other night. I didn't mean to offend you."

"Sure. Okay." *And what about René? Is that not supposed to offend me, too?* she thought hatefully, but said nothing.

"About the hayride. Are you still coming?" He put his hands in his pockets. Good, that was safe. If he touched her, she didn't know what she might do.

Bethany sneezed. *Convenient*, she thought. "No, I'm getting over a cold. I shouldn't even be out here." How dare he mention the hayride!

"Oh." He sounded hurt, offended. Bethany could feel her jaw tightening to the point where she thought her teeth might rocket out of her mouth with the pressure. Offended? Who had the right to be offended here? Certainly not him!

"I just thought that—"

"Forget it," she snapped.

He was so close now that she could smell the sweetness of his skin. *If he touches me,* she thought, *I'm a goner.* He said her name softly and she groaned inside, stepping away quickly. "I said I'm fine. We have work to do." She grabbed the cauldron, pushed past him and marched inside, keeping her head down, never looking into his eyes.

"You've been crying," said Nam, sympathy in her voice.

Tillie took one look at Bethany's face, and said, "You didn't talk to him, did you?"

Bethany set the cauldron on the coffee table. "Yeah, I talked to him, I told him to come inside."

"Then where is he?" asked Nam, peering around Bethany.

Bethany straightened. "He was right behind me."

"He's not there now," said Tillie, walking out of the family room and into the kitchen. "In fact," she called, "he's not anywhere."

They heard a car roar out of the driveway.

Nam frowned. "My Venus was not well aspected today. No wonder all this junk is going on in my social life."

Tillie groaned.

They tried to burn the Witch's ladder in the cauldron, adding angelica and jinx-removing powder. The mess didn't want to light, and the long-stick matches kept going out. Frustrated, Bethany finally took the cauldron outside and added some charcoal lighter fluid.

"Are you sure that's going to be enough fluid to make it burn?" asked Nam, standing behind her.

"Beats me," said Bethany, "I never use the stuff. My dad does all the grilling."

Tillie shook her head. "You know, this is dangerous. A relative of mine put too much fluid on the grill one time? And he was in the hospital for months with third-degree burns. He'll never be the same. His face looks like a monster in a horror film. I think you put on way too much."

Bethany was still so angry, she never heard her. She lit the match, there was a horrid *woosh!* and Tillie was yanking Bethany back by her long hair, the two of them hitting the patio with a heavy thud, cracking elbows on the flagstone. She missed singeing her eyebrows by a millisecond. How many times had Ramona told her to be careful with fire, and here she sat on Tillie's chest, her heart beating wildly because she was angry, threw on too much fluid, and nearly torched her whole head. Dumb. Dumb. Dumb.

Tillie, eyes wide, pushed at Bethany's backside. "You weigh a ton," she said in a strangled voice. "One thing was for sure, whoever made that Witch's ladder certainly knew what they were doing. You almost turned into a teenaged marshmallow."

"Magick had nothing to do with it," said Bethany, standing up and rubbing her elbows. "Just sheer stupidity." She reached over and gave Tillie a hand. "Thanks."

"No problem, but you might want to do some butt-reducing exercises."

"Very funny."

"We should have cast a ritual circle," said Nam. "And we didn't. We just rushed out here."

"That'll teach us," said Tillie, examining a sizeable rip in the seat of her blue jeans.

"A ritual circle doesn't protect you if you don't use your common sense," said Bethany, watching the fire licking toward the sky.

Nam puckered her lips. "Sidney would have remembered to cast the circle. I should have paid more attention to Venus square Venus."

"If you don't knock it off, Nam, my Venus is going to punch your Venus in the nose," growled Bethany.

"Your Venus is lovesick," said Nam.

"No, her Venus is a scorned woman," remarked Tillie.

Bethany threw up her hands. "Enough already!"

The other two snickered.

"I fail to see the humor in any of this!" shouted Bethany, swallowing her own giggle. They watched the fire dwindle to a few erratic sparks, then sputter and die. They doused the entire mess with vinegar, then carried it off Bethany's property, dumping the evil goo in a ditch, covering the jumble of ashes with clumps of wet dirt and leaves.

"I'm hungry," whined Tillie as they went back in the house.

Nam wandered into the family room. "Sidney's backpack is gone. Guess he came back and got it."

Bethany stuck her hand in her jacket pocket, her fingers brushing against cold metal. The key! She'd forgotten all about it. She pulled it out and looked at it in the kitchen light.

"What have you got there?" asked Tillie.

"A key, and you won't believe how I got it," said Bethany.

Nam walked in the kitchen. "What's that?"

"Bethany found a key," said Tillie.

"Where'd you get it?" asked Nam.

"A bird."

Tillie leaned forward. "As in one with wings?"

Bethany nodded. "Told you that you wouldn't believe me."

Nam cocked her head. "I've seen keys like that before."

"Yeah, like when you were a little girl," said Bethany.

Nam's slender eyebrow rose. "No, I saw it recently. Let me think . . . I know! At the orchard. That's the kind of keys they use there. Tad had one on a keychain. I remember seeing it and thinking no one used that kind of lock anymore."

"We need to do some snooping at the orchard," said Tillie.

Bethany sighed. "I called this afternoon after I got home. Clarence answered the phone. He said that although the family was grateful that we helped Cricket, there are no jobs available at this time. We can't work at the Bindart place, even if we wanted to."

"That's just bull," said Tillie. "We have to get back to the orchard."

Nam shook her head vehemently. "Oh no, not me. I'm not prowling around out there tonight. Nothing doing! I'm not ruining another pair of shoes. These cost me over sixty dollars!"

"Only a fool would pay that kind of money for those kind of shoes," said Tillie, looking down her nose at Nam's sparkling crimson footwear. "I thought you were—"

"Saving money," mimicked Nam. "I just couldn't resist."

"If you don't watch out, your parents will cut up your credit cards," chided Bethany.

Nam wrinkled her nose. "Over my dead body."

"Knowing your father," said Tillie, "it may come to that." Her face grew animated. "I just thought of something! We don't have to go tonight, we can go on the hayride tomorrow. It's sponsored by Bindart's Farm! We can just go along with all the others, and then slip away. No one will miss us. Sidney said all the employees from the bank and their families are invited. We'll just get lost in the crowd!"

Bethany leaned against the kitchen counter, crossing her arms over her chest. "I will not go on that hayride! I will not be humiliated!"

"Ever hear of fighting for your man?" asked Tillie.

"I've got a baseball bat," offered Nam.

"Disgusting," retorted Bethany. "I will not lower myself."

"Ooh!" chirped Nam. "This could be exciting! What are we looking for?"

"It will *not* be exciting, I am *not* going!"

"You mean you'd let us go after a killer . . . alone?" asked Tillie.

Bethany smashed her face in her hands and dragged her fingers down her skin. "I do not believe you are doing this to me. Besides, I already told him I wasn't going. I have no idea what time . . . and, the question of the evening . . . what will we be looking for?"

Tillie waved her hand. "The lock that fits that key, to start."

Nam looked at the key. "Couldn't we just . . . you know . . . go to the mall?"

Bethany tried her best, but she couldn't sleep. Thoughts of Sidney, René, Cricket . . . she sighed, rolled out of bed, and blew her nose. Nothing like a cold to make you miserable. As much as she wanted to ruin René's life, she knew that it would be wrong. Besides, the threat of losing something else to random magick wasn't the most appealing thought. There was something, however, that she could do about the hit-and-run on her car. She'd stop at the garage that housed the totaled Camaro tomorrow before school started.

Chapter 15

Wednesday evening

Tillie picked up Nam and Bethany in her rattle-trap Toyota, the muffler growling like an ailing polar bear. "I'm sure no one will be suspicious," said Tillie sarcastically, "seeing as how we are all dressed in black. Ahem."

"I didn't want to stand out," said Bethany.

"Me neither," said Nam, adjusting her black fedora.

Tillie raised an eyebrow, looking at Nam in the rearview mirror. "That'll be the day."

Bethany fastened her seatbelt. "Great. We look like a Wiccan hit team." The muffler belched and the car backfired. "Why is the passenger window down?"

"Broken," said Tillie. "My little brother thought he could fix it, and the whole window slid down in the door right before we left. I couldn't get it out." She turned the car heater up full blast. "Sorry."

"This is embarrassing," said Nam, clutching her hat as the car bucked and chugged through the intersection.

"You could have driven," said Tillie, turning off the highway and onto the country roads.

"And use my car?" said Nam. "Not after what happened to Bethany's Camaro. My insurance is already higher than I can afford. My insurance rates are so high you could take a stairway to heaven and still not reach them. Besides, my honorable father forbids me to drive at night unless I'm going to or from work."

"Ah, the real reason," said Tillie.

Nam made a face, and said, "Did you remember to bring the key, Bethany?"

Bethany waived the key in the air. "Right here."

Tillie hit a pothole and the key flew from her fingers, spinning out of the open window into the cold night air. "I *had* the key," said Bethany, her voice dropping to the miniscule range.

Tillie jerked to a stop, then backed up the car.

"We'll never find it in the dark!" wailed Nam, looking at the mess of rotted and tangled weeds by the roadside.

"I knew this was a bad idea," moaned Bethany. "Take me home."

Tillie put the car back in gear. "Nothing doing. We're going. Key or no key."

Bethany fumbled in her purse, looking for tissues, pulling out a small red bag in the process.

"What's that?" asked Tillie. "In the red bag? That's a conjuring bag, isn't it?"

"Keep your eyes on the road," complained Nam. "You just drove over the double yellow line."

"Next time, you drive," said Tillie. "Extravagant insurance or no. So, what's in the bag?"

Bethany scowled, the wind whipping around her head from the open window. She sneezed. "I'm sure to get double pneumonia." She tugged on her coat collar. "I'm going to get good and sick out of all this, I just know it."

"Good and sick in the same sentence," said Tillie. "Interesting thought. How does one get good and sick at the same time? Good at what?"

"Getting sick!" yelled Nam from the back seat.

Bethany held up the red flannel bag, holding on-to it tightly for fear it would whiz out the open window after the key. "It's to get whoever hit my car."

"Cool," said Nam, sliding forward on the back seat as far as her seatbelt would allow. She peeked over Bethany's shoulder, making strangulated sounds. "What's in it?"

"I couldn't sleep last night," said Bethany, "so I wrote out a spell. I put it together early this morn-ing. I've got a piece of tiger-eye for truth, some crushed rosemary so that the act sits heavily on their mind, a feather to represent the Goddess of Justice, Maat, and little pieces from my car . . . then I prayed that Spirit would lead us to the person that hit my Camaro, and that justice would be done."

"How'd you get pieces of your Camaro?" asked Tillie, turning the car onto Old Mill Road. It was so bumpy the words vibrated through the interior of the car.

"I walked down to the garage this morning. They thought I was nuts, but they let me have some. I chose a piece that had the black paint on it from the Bronco. I was lucky, they were just getting ready to haul the Camaro to the junkyard."

Nam strained against the seatbelt. "So do you think it will act like a magickal homing device?"

Bethany laughed. "Hardly, but I thought I'd bring it along tonight. I mean, what could it hurt?"

The orchard looked like a fairy retreat. Small twinkling lights hung from the front of the store and the grading shed, trailing down an access road into the orchard. Wind chimes ornamented the nearest trees, filling the air with soft, enchanted sounds.

"Wow!" said Nam, chewing on a wad of bubble gum. "Would you look at that!"

"You know, if they worked this right, they could do more of these all through Thanksgiving vacation and the Christmas season to make a little extra money," remarked Tillie.

"Maybe enough to at least get their bank loan out of arrears," whispered Bethany. "Wonder who thought of this?"

Cricket stood at the attic window, wrapped in a warm comforter, staring down at the people milling in and around the store parking lot. She couldn't believe the wonderful job her mother had done getting ready for this big night. Her father was going to talk to Sidney's dad about the bank loan. She sighed. Where was Leslee?

A small car chugged into the parking lot, blowing steam and making a terrible racket. Several people turned around to watch three girls dressed in black emerge from the car. One tugged on a black fedora. The Witches! If they were here, maybe everything would be okay.

The back of her neck prickled and she turned around. Zee stood just inside her bedroom door, staring at her.

"What do you want?" she asked, trying to keep the fear from her voice. He was big and smelled from the heavy exertion of working in the orchard, and he hardly said anything to anyone except when her father told him to. She hated him because he had done something with Leslee. She was sure it was something bad. She should have said something to the Witches, but she was too embarrassed to spill that family secret. She'd probably told them too much already, but what choice did she have?

Zee just stood there.

Her fear flared into anger. "Either you say something, do something, or get out!" she said. "And when I figure out what you did with Leslee, I'm going to make you pay!"

Zee cocked his head, as if contemplating, or maybe he didn't understand. *He could be slow,* thought Cricket. *Maybe mentally challenged.* She'd never thought of that. In all his years on the farm, he had never, ever spoken directly to her. He was just a big guy who wore a red bandanna like a badge of honor. A mere shade in the brilliant garden of life. She chewed on a thumbnail. Studying Shakespeare must twist your brain in poetic ways. Next she'd be shouting soliloquies, which she doubted very much would help her now.

She heard the sound of a paper bag crinkling and she looked down. Zee held a big bag tightly in his hands, folding and unfolding the top.

Maybe he had a knife in there, or a gun . . . or . . .

"I brung this to ya," he said, but he didn't move and he didn't produce the contents of the bag; instead, he kept looking at the floor, rolling and unrolling the edges.

Cricket said nothing.

"I didn't hurt Leslee," he said. "She's the one who wanted me to give you these. I don't think it's a good idea, but she insisted."

Cricket's heart did a double pound. "Leslee? Is she okay?"

"She's right fine."

Cricket waited, but he didn't offer any more information. Evidently he wasn't much on explanations. The bag continued to whisper in the stillness of the attic. Cricket took a step forward. Zee did not move one way or the other.

"She's not in the hospital or anything?"

Zee shook his head. "I took her there. They fixed her up. Wasn't much. She's home. She's happy."

Home? Happy? Cricket felt a little dizzy and sat on the edge of her bed. "She's here, now?"

"No. Home. Happy."

"But this is her home!"

The bag continued to rustle. "No."

Squeals and shouts of laughter drifted up from the orchard parking lot.

"I drive the tractor that pulls the wagon," said Zee. "Clarence will drive the other one."

Cricket shook her head. She didn't care who drove what tractor. It was her sister she wanted to know about. She put her head in her hand, feeling lightheaded, but she forged on. "Zee," she said patiently, "where is Leslee?"

"Leslee and the baby are home."

Cricket's head snapped up. "She had her baby?"

"No, not yet. Everyone is safe. She doesn't want you to worry. You can't tell anyone I stopped by to see you. I brung you these . . . from her . . . sort of . . . but they are mine." He gently set the bag by the edge of the bed, but his manner was so odd that Cricket didn't immediately move to touch it.

Zee started for the door, then turned. "I won't be seeing you no more after tonight and I'm mighty sorry that I hurt that boy in the barn, but I thought . . . correct that . . . I didn't think. Again, I'm sorry."

Cricket could feel her brow wrinkling in puzzlement. "I don't understand. Are you going away?"

"I can't work here no more." He slipped out of the bedroom without another word.

If that bag is not three-dimensional, said Cricket to herself, *then I know this whole thing is a result of a fever, and I should just go back to bed and put the covers over my head.*

As they walked to the edges of the crowd several heads turned to stare at them, but the entrance of two shiny John Deere tractors trundling through the parking lot made such a commotion that most people lost interest in the Witches, though a few of the adults spewed snide remarks and purposely made a show of clinging to their children. Bethany was sure their actions were more out of spite than real fear.

"Where's Sidney?" asked Nam, adjusting the black fedora on her head.

Tillie craned her neck. "Over there," she pointed, her gold bracelets tinkling down her arm.

"Is he alone?" asked Nam, chewing viciously on her bubble gum.

Tillie looked again. "No. René is beside him. No, she's hanging all over him. She's wearing a red sweater. Bright red! Now she's saying something in his ear. Okay . . . okay . . . now she's . . . oh, my . . . well. She's with him, anyway."

Bethany felt her shoulders tense, anger rising in her throat, pulling at the tendons in her neck, tickling her ears. "I'm leaving."

Tillie grabbed her arm. "Don't be ridiculous. You can't leave. I'm driving. You'd have to walk. It's over ten miles."

Nam stood in front of her. "Besides, the hayride is just an excuse to be here," she said, yelling over the crowd. "Either we're going to snoop—"

"Lower your voice," said Bethany, as a few people turned to stare. "Your big mouth got me in trouble once before. You're not at a hog-calling contest, you know."

Nam tilted her chin, narrowing her eyes. "Meow!" she said.

More people turned to stare, but Mrs. Bindart moved through the gathering with helium-filled balloons for the children and there was a mad rush toward the brightly colored bobbing plastic tethered to her outstretched hand. Some of the balloons were shaped like animals.

"I want the canary," said Tillie.

"Oh, that would look cute, a Witch dressed in black playing detective while pulling along a big yellow bird balloon. How utterly innocuous," hissed Bethany.

Nam dropped her voice to a whisper, "We came here to help Cricket. So, let's do it. When they all leave, we'll lag behind. Check out the grading shed, the equipment shed, and then we'll move to the migrant's house, the old barn, and the garage back there." She motioned toward the white clapboard house. "We've got to turn up something! We'll check everywhere."

Tillie pouted.

"Are we only looking for the lock that fits the key Bethany lost?" asked Nam.

Tillie walked closer to the shadows of the parking lot, allowing distance between themselves and those loading onto the wagons. "No. Last night Sidney said we should be looking for the black Bronco. Someone may be hiding it on the property. We figure out who the Bronco belongs to, then maybe we can work through to the reason behind all the things happening here."

"Sidney? When did he say this?" asked Bethany.

"When you were trying to recite Edgar Allan Poe to that dumb bird," said Nam.

"Why are we listening to him?" asked Bethany. "He's a cheater! A slime!"

"He's smarter than a bird," said Tillie.

Nam grabbed Bethany by the arms and shook her. "Bethany! Forget you're angry with Sidney. Can we just stick to the subject? We are looking for the black Bronco, not Sidney. We know where he is . . . oops. I didn't mean that the way it sounded."

Bethany slapped her thigh with her hand. "Okay. Fine! So what if the Bronco and the other things aren't related? What then?"

"Be a mud puddle," complained Nam. "Whoever killed the rabbits and clunked Cricket on the head probably owns the Bronco. Even if it has nothing to do with Alice, at least we've got something solved! You filed a police report on your accident. We can get that person for hit-and-run."

Bethany nodded grudgingly. There was a thought.

"In the meantime," said Tillie, "we can try to find the lock that fits the invisible key, and also look for magickal paraphernalia. You know, herbs, a cauldron, maybe a wand, something that would tell us who is trying to play God with magick. It might be someone different than the owner of the Bronco, or they may be one and the same. It won't hurt to look."

"Tally ho!" yelled someone from a wagon. The tractors growled and jerked, pulling the wagons toward the magically lit access road. Giggles, laughter, and howls of delight feathered through the November evening. Bethany craned her neck. The couple in the back of the second wagon looked familiar. Bethany squinted. It was René and Sidney, René's red-clad arms curled around Sidney's neck. Gag me. René was so dead! Her hand flew to her mouth. No, no, she didn't mean that in the realistic sense. She dug her nails into her palms. Once you knew thoughts were things, you could never go back.

They crept around behind the store, peeking in the office windows and scurrying across open ground. The grading shed door was open, lights blazing, but no one was there. The store, too, was open, with Mrs. Bindart behind the counter, hoping, Bethany supposed, that the bank employees would stop in when the ride was done to pick up produce, honey, cider, or any of the other country delectables.

The interior of the equipment shed was also exposed and well lit, with a migrant worker lounging beside the doors, waiting for the return of the tractors and wagons. The area was open, no hidden walls and no odd cubicles. The garage beside the workers' white house didn't have a lock. A battered truck, one compact car, and an old Buick with fire-engine flames airbrushed on the side. Definitely not Bronco material.

"Okay," Tillie said, crouching at the back of the store. "There's nothing in the store, the grading shed, or the equipment shed. The only other place big enough in this area that could hold the Bronco would be the family garage, and Cricket would know if there was a Bronco there, which we will assume there isn't." The large willow tree afforded them minimal cover, but with the long shadows of the store, it was about the best place to confer.

"There's that modern barn," said Bethany. "I think it's up on the north ridge. But there wasn't any sign of a Bronco when we were there, and Cricket said she goes there a lot."

Nam blew a large bubble, then popped it with a black fingernail. "Yeah, but remember she said she hadn't been there in a while, and then there was that oil stain on the floor with the kitty litter sprinkled on it? Someone could be hiding the Bronco in that barn. I remember seeing a black Bronco driving past the cemetery the day we were there. It slowed down when Cricket pulled that old station wagon next to your Camaro. That could explain why it wasn't in the barn when we got there."

"Because it was following us," said Tillie.

"Lucky break for the driver," remarked Bethany.

"Why didn't you say anything before, ninny?" asked Tillie, lightly punching Nam's arm.

"I dunno. Just came to me now, I guess," replied Nam, blowing another bubble.

"If you had a brain, you'd be dangerous," said Tillie.

"I'm lethal," remarked Nam. "If you remember, I have the best batting average on the girls' softball team."

Bethany leaned against the building. "Aren't there any other structures on the property big enough to house that Bronco?"

Tillie drew out a piece of folded paper, flapped it a few times, then opened it up, squinting at the small print.

"What's that?" asked Nam.

"It's a list of buildings on the property," said Tillie. "Sidney got it from his father and brought it along last night. He gave it to me while you were outside. I don't know how he got it and I don't care. Says here there's also several cottages and some have garages."

Bethany looked at her watch. "We've been searching for over forty-five minutes. They'll all be back soon. Those houses could be on the other side of the mountain! How do we know where to look next?"

"Wait, I've got an idea," said Tillie. "Shine your flashlight on the ground and give me that red flannel bag you made." They watched as Tillie placed the conjuring bag on the ground first, then the paper on top. "Hand me your Witches' Night Out necklace," she said to Nam.

Nam reached under her shirt. "It's gone!" she wailed.

"Shh!" cautioned Bethany, "someone may hear you. Maybe you just forgot to put it on."

"No, no!" cried Nam. "I would never lose that. I take very good care of it, because it represents my bond with you guys."

Bethany dug under her black turtleneck, extricating her own necklace. "Here," she said to Tillie. "Use mine. Nam, don't worry, if it is lost we'll just get you another one."

"But what if there's a magickal meaning that I lost it?" said Nam, her eyes wide. "What if it means I'm not supposed to be in the group?" Her lower lip trembled.

"Don't be an idiot," snapped Tillie, dangling the pendant over the list. "We couldn't be a group without you. Sometimes you drive me crazy, but that doesn't mean I don't think of you as a sister. You can't put a mystical meaning to everything.

Like Bethany said the other night, sometimes shit just happens. Bethany, you hold the light. Now everyone shut up and concentrate."

Tillie sat back on her haunches. "Show me yes," she said. After a minute or so the necklace drifted back and forth horizontally. "Good," she said. "Show me no." The necklace drifted in a vertical, repetitive motion, quicker this time. "Show me I don't know." The pendant twirled in a circle. "Great! Now, let's go through the list."

"This could take forever," muttered Nam, snapping her gum.

"Not really," said Tillie, "we've already checked most of these places. I'll just list off the ones we haven't been to. It won't take long, I promise."

Nam blew a particularly large bubble that promptly exploded on her face. "Sorry," she said weakly, pulling strings of bubble gum out of her hair.

Chapter 16

From her attic vantage point, Cricket watched the bank employees and their families load into the wagons. Her breath lightly fogged the window, and she rubbed the moisture away with the corner of her comforter. She didn't see the Witches get on the wagons, and wondered if they might have opted to do some sleuthing. Maybe she should sit here, sort of like a lookout, in case they got into trouble. She eyed the paper bag at the end of her bed, but made no move to touch it. She wanted to know, but then again, she didn't. After twenty minutes of staring out at the deserted parking lot her eyes grew weary, so she turned back to the paper bag.

She dumped the contents on the bed.

Books. Just paperback books. Some were for little kids and others for teens. Why would her sister send her a bunch of books? She looked at them closer. Her father would never allow these novels in the house. They weren't religious and they weren't Shakespeare. All were from the same author, Zeddadiah Linquist.

She flipped to the back cover of a teen novel. Her jaw dropped and she seriously thought that she was going into cardiac arrest. Zeddadiah was Zee! There was his picture—though all cleaned up and in new clothes, it was him alright. And in the photo he was smiling! Zee never, ever smiled. The caption underneath read: "Zeddadiah Linquist, author of more than thirty books for children and young adults. He lives in rural Pennsylvania with his wife, Leslee, and their two-year-old daughter."

Cricket sat on the edge of her bed, her mouth working, her eyes twirling around in her head. When did she have the baby? Cricket thought back . . . two years ago, right around the time of the fire, Leslee had gone away for a few months. Cricket's ears caught a muffled sound on the stairs, then actual footsteps. Frantically she shoved the books back in the bag and hid them under her bed.

"Okay," said Tillie. "The cottages seem clear, except for this one." She pointed her finger at the last house listed. "I'm getting an I-don't-know answer. According to the description on Sidney's list, I think it's down the access road and to the left. The trouble is, I'm also getting the same sort of answer for the barn that Cricket took us to. I don't get it."

"No solid affirmative answers, I take it," said Bethany. "Great." She put the necklace back on, not bothering to stick it underneath her sweater.

"Bummer," said Nam. "We can't be two places at once, and we're running out of time."

"We could split up," suggested Tillie.

"Bad idea," said Bethany. "If whoever has done all these things finds us snooping, we could be in danger. Three are hard to beat, but one?" She shook her head. "Look, we know Alice is dead and that someone hurt Cricket. They tried to take us out back in Cedar Crest. This person will get physical if they have to."

The trio stood there, staring at one another. No one could come up with a solution that didn't split them apart.

"Bethany and I will go together," said Sidney.

The girls spun in unison. Nam squealed, her gum popping out of her mouth and flying to the ground. "I wish you would stop sneaking up on people like that," she said, her tiny hand clutched to her chest. "You're taking years off our lives."

Sidney grinned. "It's the Native American in me. Just can't help it. We are fleet of foot and oh so cool."

"Barf-ola," shot Bethany, her lip curling in disdain. "Tell me, where's your girlfriend?" The shadows were so deep behind the store she could hardly make out his face. She was tempted to shine the flashlight in his eyes and blind him, but thought better of it. In fact, she snapped it off. If Sidney found them, the hayride might be over, though she didn't hear anyone out in the parking lot. Still, it was dumb to keep the flashlight on—she should have thought to turn it off earlier.

Sidney faced Bethany. His voice sounded odd, strange. "She's standing right here, I think."

"Where?" asked Bethany. "You don't mean you dragged René into this, did you?"

Sidney shifted his feet. "René? What has she got to do with it?"

"Duh!" said Tillie, smacking her forehead with her palm, her bracelets jangling. "You only called her and asked her to the hayride. You only went with her on said hayride with her arms wrapped around you like an octopus. I mean, not that it's any of my business."

Sidney shook his head, then turned to Bethany. "Let me get this straight. You're not mad at me because of the other night? Because I kissed you?"

"He kissed you? Ooh!" said Nam, clapping her hands together. "You didn't say anything about kissing, Bethany!"

Bethany was now absolutely, positively mortified.

"And you're not mad over what I said about your mother?" Sidney went on.

"What about her mama?" snarled Tillie.

Sidney ignored her. "You're mad about René?"

Bethany said nothing. She was sure if she opened her mouth they would all die on the spot from her killing breath, so vile were her thoughts, so horrid was her hatred that her stomach felt like a cauldron of acid.

Sidney threw back his head and laughed.

"Shh!" squealed Nam. "No one's supposed to know we're here!"

Sidney lowered his voice. "Yeah. I noticed. The all-black thing is an interesting touch. Cute hat,

Nam. The fedora really does it for you. People on the hayride were commenting about the evil Witches. I'm sure Sunday services for many of them will be quite inspiring."

"Oh, no," groaned Tillie.

Sidney cleared his throat. "René means nothing to me, Bethany. I can explain."

Tillie flapped her hand in the air, her gold bracelets tinkling. "Oh, this ought to be good."

"Seriously," said Sidney. "René's father called my dad the other night. Mr. Farmore is my father's vice president. He wanted to know if I could escort René because he doesn't want her around Judd Reese, and her father couldn't come tonight. My father volunteered me. And yes, my father and I have had a long and interesting discussion about that point, but I don't want to get into it here."

Tillie surveyed him suspiciously. "You didn't personally ask René out?"

"No."

"You didn't go to her house the other night?" asked Bethany.

"Who gave you a crazy idea like that?"

"I'm gonna get that Charlene," said Tillie.

"Before or after I pulverize René?" asked Bethany.

"Who's Charlene?"

"Never mind," said Tillie. "I'll handle her later."

"I wasn't happy about it because I'm dating Bethany," said Sidney, "and also because René is a troublemaker. She has a bad habit of twisting things and then, when everyone is caught in her web of deceit, she squirms out of it. I've known her since I was a little kid. Some day, if we're lucky, she'll do herself in."

Bethany didn't know whether to believe him and feel relieved, or to disbelieve him and tell him what a lying sack of excrement he was. She remembered Ramona's warning about gossip and felt foolish. "I should have known," she said. "The day I was told you were dating René, Ramona told me about gossip. I should have listened to her. She was telling me right to my face that it wasn't true, and I missed her point completely."

Sidney moved closer to her. Her first thought? Step back. One problem, the store wall was in the way. He pinned Bethany against the wall, one outstretched arm on either side of her stiffened shoulders. "You're the only girl for me."

"Takes my breath away," said Tillie.

"Time to swoon, Bethany," giggled Nam.

Bethany opened her mouth to protest, but his sweet, warm lips crushed her own. What the heck. She grabbed his waist and leaned in.

Tillie cleared her throat. "Excuse me, campers. We have a mystery to solve? You can lock lips later."

"Who's there?" asked Cricket. The footsteps stopped in front of her door, but no one knocked. "I said, who's there?"

Silence.

She shivered and pulled the comforter closer under her chin. In the distance she could hear the tractors returning with their load of happy hayriders. The house sat silent. Creaking. The heater kicked on, the pipes clanking, steam escaping from the radiator, and she imagined her room filled with the hot repulsive breath of poisonous snakes.

Slowly, the door swung open.

"What are *you* doing here?" she asked in surprise.

"Okay," said Tillie. "Nam and I will check the fancy barn, and Sidney and Bethany will go to that last cottage on the list. I can hear the tractors, so they're coming back. We should get going. Bethany, do you have your cell phone?"

"I forgot mine," said Sidney.

"Me, too," said Nam. "Sorry. It's charging in my bedroom."

"Great place for it," snapped Tillie. "You get a cell phone for emergencies . . . oh, never mind."

"Wait a minute," said Nam. "Where's yours?"

Embarrassment flowed across Tillie's face. "My mother borrowed it."

"We are lousy detectives," said Sidney.

Bethany dipped inside her coat pocket. "I've got mine." She twirled the flashlight in her other hand. "Here, you'll probably need this. The cottage will most likely be lit, and with the fairy lights, we can keep off the access road but still see to get there." She handed the light over to Tillie, accidentally shining it in Sidney's eyes.

"Hey!" said Tillie, stepping closer. "What happened to your face!"

Sidney delicately touched his right eye. "Oh. That."

"What a shiner!" exclaimed Nam, peering up at him.

"Who did that to you!?" asked Bethany.

Sidney let out a strangled laugh. "I ran into Judd."

"Boy, I'll say," said Tillie. "I hope he looks worse."

"He does. René is nursing his wounds. My father was there, though, so it's cool. Judd jumped me and pulled me off the wagon while we were making the turn beyond the lights, thinking no one would see. My dad doesn't miss anything. Suddenly the wagons stopped, and I sort of . . . defended myself. René sat there laughing until her precious boy-toy went down for the count. That's how I know she set me up. My dad sent me back to have my eye looked at, so he won't miss me."

"Man, what a monster," said Tillie. "I never did like that girl."

"Yeah, but what about your eye?" said Nam. "Maybe somebody should look at it."

"Later," said Sidney.

"At least let Bethany work on it. She's good at emergency healings," said Nam.

Tillie pulled Nam's arm. "We haven't got time!"

"She's right," said Bethany. "As soon as we leave here, you should go to the emergency room. Just to make sure."

"I don't have a headache and my vision isn't blurred," he said, "but if it will make you happy, I'll stop by the Doc in a Box on the way into town and have them look at it, okay?"

Bethany nodded and they set off in the direction of the cottage while Nam and Tillie moved stealthily across a small, stubbled field, heading uphill toward the modernized barn.

"Maybe we should just drive over," said Tillie.

"In that heap?" asked Nam. "With your hair, your bracelets, and that rubber-band-mobile, you're like a full marching band. We wouldn't be able to take anyone by surprise. Why didn't you remind me to bring my baseball bat?"

"What, bad aspects again?" grunted Tillie, leaping over a log at the edge of the dark field.

"In all the excitement," said Nam with a sheepish grin, "I forgot to check them."

"I don't want to look at anything but you," said Sidney, stopping just shy of the fairy lights along the access road. "How could you ever think I would hurt you like that? I was going to explain last night, but you got mad and went in the house. I was going to tell you about René, but you ignored me all day. I guess I lost my temper. I couldn't understand what was eating at you."

"Just forget it," said Bethany, encircling his waist with her arms. "I'm sorry I jumped to conclusions."

"Promise me that you'll never do that again," said Sidney. "That we'll always talk things out."

Bethany put her head on his chest. "It's hard for me to talk about personal things."

He stroked her hair. "I know, but I don't want anything to ever come between us like that." He held her close, their hearts beating together. After a moment, he said, "I need to talk to you about your mother . . . "

Bethany's arms grew rigid.

"Not now. Some other time. When you are ready. Okay?"

Bethany sighed and nodded. "Okay. Sometime."

He kissed her again and she thought her whole world would spin upside down. "You'll get my cold," she said.

"As if I care," he mumbled.

"We're supposed to be sleuthing," she said.

"Oh, yeah. Right." But he didn't immediately let go.

They circled the last cottage. A single light burned in what looked like a back bedroom. Together, they scuttled under the window, listening for movement inside.

Nothing.

A dog started to bark, but it wasn't close. Probably at another cottage across the property. Slowly, Bethany raised her head and peered in the window. The shades were only drawn three-quarters of the way down, so she could see most of the room. A bed, compact disc player, and female clothes thrown everywhere. A teen's room. It didn't look like anyone was hiding under the bed. A closet door hung open, gaping at them, filled with a tumble of clothes, shoes, a tennis racket, and dirty underwear.

"Whoever lives here," said Bethany, "definitely couldn't count neatness as a strong point."

Sidney raised himself up, looking in as well. "There," he whispered. "Over there. Doesn't that look like an altar to you?"

Bethany squinted. "Sure does. Who lives here?"

"I have no idea. The properties just list an address and the holder, which is the Bindart family. Tenants' names weren't included."

Bethany tried the window, and it slid up a few inches. "Lucky day! How about this," said Bethany. "You knock on the door. See who lives here. Use your injured eye as an excuse if you have to. Meanwhile, I'll crawl in through the window and get a better look."

"Bad idea," said Sidney. "What if there's more than one person in the house?"

"I can handle myself," said Bethany. "Just go!"

Sidney duck-walked back around the side of the house. She could hear him knocking on the door. Slowly, she slid the window open, then hefted herself up on the sill, silently cursing her bulky coat. She dropped in the room, knocking over a ceramic figurine, which broke into a thousand pieces on the hardwood floor. She held her breath, but no one came flying into the room. Thank the Goddess the bedroom door was shut. Maybe the occupants were so busy with Sidney, they didn't hear her.

Head cocked for any sound of discovery, she moved across the room to get a better look at the altar. What she saw made her sick. Red candles, love oils, herbs for passion, some bottom-feeder chapbook about getting your man using unethical practices, rawhide, red feathers, and a large cauldron filled with truly evil-smelling stuff. Bethany wrinkled her nose with disgust. If she could smell it through this head cold, it must be bad. All this time the girls thought that the folk charms were for hexing, when in fact they were unscrupulous baubles for love. How many times had Ramona told them that there were several uses to each charm, talisman, or amulet? If she'd just shown Ramona the tanglefoot and the Witch's ladder, the Creole housekeeper would have known exactly what they were for.

Whose room was this? She looked around quickly, riffling through papers and books. There was even a backpack here, but it was empty. She flung it aside. Ah! There! A diary! She lunged for the little green book with gold lettering as the bedroom door creaked open.

Shit! This is it. Crap. Crap. She looked at the moving door in terror, gauging the distance between the window and her position. Too far! Too far! She shoved the diary under her shirt and crouched down, the heavy cardboard cover of the book digging into her stomach.

Chapter 17

"Bethany?"

"Sidney?" She rose from her crouched position, the circulation returning to her stomach as she adjusted the sharp edge of the diary. "What are you doing in here?" she whispered.

"No one's home and the front door was open."

She swallowed, trying to calm her beating heart. She was beginning to think twice about this sleuthing thing. This was the first time she'd actually broken into anyone's home, and something about that made her feel dirty. "I found this," she said, removing the diary from under her shirt.

"Interesting hiding place," he said.

She grinned thinly. "Cute."

"So do we know who lives here?" asked Sidney.

"Not yet, but what we all thought were magicks for curses were a desperate attempt to bring love."

Sidney eyed the altar. His fingers ran over perfumes, a bowl of fresh rose petals, and red candles. He raised a small vial to the light, squinting to read the label. "Passion Oil," he said, unscrewing the top and taking a whiff. "You ever do any of this stuff?

Oh, yuck. What's in the cauldron? Smells like dead body parts."

"It's an herbal mixture," said Bethany.

"This is love magick?"

"Get serious," said Bethany.

He turned and grinned. "I don't know, I'm feeling pretty bewitched right now. If I put some of this passion oil at the hollow of your throat, could I nuzzle you?"

Bethany smacked him with the diary and it flew out of her hand, landing open on the bed. The vial of passion oil shot through the air, spattered on the wall, and landed upside down in the cauldron. "Shoot!" said Bethany. "Not only have we messed up the working, now someone will know we were here. I hope adding passion oil to that concoction won't do any harm." She walked over to the bed. "I don't believe it," said Bethany, moving closer to the book. "This is Alice's diary! But I don't remember Alice living on the farm. The police gave a different address, I'm sure of it."

Sidney picked up the book and thumbed through it. "Looks like she had the hots for Tad Bindart. Isn't that Cricket's twin brother?"

A blob of black torqued through the window and both teens ducked. "Hey!" yelled Sidney. "It's a raven!"

The bird perched on the bedrail, staring at them.

"Do you think he bites?" asked Sidney.

"And I should know?" retorted Bethany. She thought of the lost key and looked at the bedroom door. An old lock. An old key!

The bird flew over and sat on top of a pink and blue jewelry box at the edge of a dusty dresser, then flew back across the bed. Keeping one eye on the bird, Sidney slowly walked over to the box and opened it. Bethany followed him, peering at the contents. "That's Nam's jewelry! Her WNO pendant, her ring, her amber necklace, her bracelet. . . ." She hesitated, then grabbed Nam's things out of the box and shoved them in her pants pocket. Technically this was stealing, but is stealing something from the stealer to give back to the steal-ee wrong? Well, she'd worry about the ethics later.

Headlights glanced across the window.

"We'd better get out of here," said Bethany, scrambling toward the window. "It could be someone from the hayride taking a short cut home, or it could be the people that live here."

"Wait, just a minute," said Sidney, leafing through the diary. "Oh, man. Oh, man!"

"What?"

"We've got to get this diary to the police. I'm sure there's a clue in here as to who killed Alice. If she wrote all this personal stuff about Tad, then she's sure to mention other people. One of them may be the killer." Sidney pulled Bethany toward the window and pushed her out, dropping silently to the ground beside her, holding tightly to the diary. "Do you think the bird is a pet?" he asked.

"I don't know," she whispered as they moved away from the house. "I wish we could have stayed longer to see who lives here. I know it wasn't Alice!"

They edged around the front of the house. No cars or trucks. "Must have went past," said Sidney. "Let's check the garage. What if all these things happening aren't connected?" asked Sidney. It was the last thing he said before Janet Atkins cold-cocked him with the head of a shovel.

"So, you found the diary. I wondered how long it would take you to figure it out," said Janet, holding the shovel between herself and Bethany, her hair billowing like a dark cloud around her head. "You being the big bad Witches of the school, and all." She kicked the diary away from Sidney's fingers, retrieved it and stuffed it in her coat pocket.

Sidney groaned and tried to sit up. Janet hit him again. Bethany rushed forward, her open coat constricting her speed. Janet swung at Bethany and caught her in the stomach, the edge of the shovel slicing open a small wound on Bethany's belly. Bethany went down, hard. "You piece of garbage," muttered Bethany, slowly hauling herself up on her knees. "What do you think you're trying to prove?"

"You're trespassing," said Janet. "This is private property. I can do as I please."

Sidney moaned. "She killed Alice. Run, Bethany! Run for help."

"Killed Alice? What? Why? I'm not running. I'm not going to leave you!"

"And not just Alice," said Janet. "I helped that fire come back to life two years ago. And got rid of that nosy migrant worker, Martha Owens! Tad Bindart belongs to me and no one is going to take him away from me! I got Alice that job. She was supposed to spy on Tad for me when I wasn't around. But the jerk found true love. And can you believe it? He fell for her like a ton of bricks! Now, I couldn't have that, could I?" Before Bethany could rise completely to her feet, Janet hit Sidney again. He was so quiet, Bethany couldn't hear him breathe.

Janet cackled hysterically, turning round and round with the shovel in her hands, her yellow coat flapping in the chill November night, her hair fanning out like black flames. "And now the twin. Cricket. I've dosed her up good. She's going to die, too! Just like Alice! Die, die, die! And the only one left for him to love will be me. Me, me, me!"

"You're insane," said Bethany. *Calm. She must remain calm. Think it, be it. Think it, be it. Power of my Mother.* Rage coursed through her veins. Janet hit Bethany again with the shovel but Bethany didn't go down. *Think it, be it. Think it, be it.* She moved toward Janet. The shovel zinged across her cheek, blood flying in the cold night air.

Think it, be it.

Bethany kept moving, her fingers flexing, the raw power of her lineage coursing through her.

Janet backed away. "Just a few moments longer and Cricket will be dead. I made her drink the same poison I gave Alice. Stupid Alice. All along she thought I was making love potions for her! It was easy to overpower Cricket, but I had to be slick to get the stuff into Alice. Now, I've killed your boyfriend. You're next," hissed Janet. She swung again, the shovel connecting with Bethany's shoulder. Bethany didn't flinch.

Think it, be it.

Focus.

Forward. Moving. They were past Sidney. Past the garage, moving into the fairy lights of the access road. Janet swung the shovel, grazing Bethany's temple. Blood clouded her eye, but she didn't feel the ooze. Bethany remained upright, her hands reaching for Janet's throat. Connecting. Squeezing. The Power of the Mother.

Think it, be it.

The raven screamed overhead.

Harbinger of death.

Announcer of birth.

Bringer of initiation.

Bethany let go. To kill was wrong. Janet lurched away, stumbling over the shovel, gasping, gagging. The shovel skittered across the frozen grass, slipping into a ditch. Janet faltered, her body swinging into the access road. Bethany tried to go after her, but she stumbled and lost her shoe, the black sneaker rolling crazily on the hard grass, clunking onto the dirt road.

The black Bronco appeared, roaring over the ruts and bumps of the cold, grooved lane, taking flight at the hump, starkly haloing Janet in the slicing headlights as she raised her head first in rage, then in fear, and sending her with a snarl of agony into oblivion.

Too late, the vehicle veered and plunged headlong into the orchard, careening on two wheels and wrapping itself around an apple tree on the opposite side of the road, the blare of its horn screaming in unison with the raven flapping overhead.

And then all was silent, save for the rattling and popping of the mangled vehicle, and the sound of steam hitting the frosty air. The rancid smell of twisted metal and gas tendriled through the night.

A tire rim rolled across the road, faltered, then fell over.

A single piece of glass struck the frozen earth, pinging once, twice, before falling flat near her sneakerless foot.

Bethany struggled to the road. Janet lay broken and unmoving. No human sound emanated from the smashed Bronco.

"Shit!" Bethany said, and promptly sat down in the center of the freezing access lane, the fairy lights still dancing crazily in the tree from the impact of the Bronco. She fumbled in her coat pocket and slowly drew out the red conjuring bag. She blinked the blood out of her eyes, holding the bag by the string in front of her. It dangled there for a moment, then she tiredly dropped her arm in her lap. "Guess I finally found that black Bronco."

The raven screamed above her, then dove in, landing a few inches from her tattered sneaker. The Bronco must have rolled over it as easily as it plowed through Janet. Bethany crawled to retrieve her sneaker, careful not to look at Janet's mangled face.

She really should go look in the Bronco.

Nah.

Dear Goddess! Sidney!

Bethany slowly got to her feet. She tried to put the sneaker on, but fell over. The bird stayed with her, never too close, never too far. She jammed the sneaker on her swollen foot. Crap, must have sprained the ankle. She tried to rise again.

Her legs gave out beneath her.

"Holy Mother," she prayed. "Let me get to Sidney. Give me the strength."

She crawled across the frozen ground, blood pulsing from her temple. She could feel the slickness on her stomach. She wondered if her shoulder was fractured, it hurt so bad. She fumbled for her other coat pocket, looking for her cell phone, but it wasn't there. Even the pocket was gone, pieces hanging raggedly from her clutching fingers. "Guess I'll really have to get a new jacket," she mumbled. She groaned.

Hand over hand. Her fingers numb from the icy ground. Her muscles screaming in pain. *I've been hurt worse than this on the hockey field,* she said to herself. *I can do this. I can make it.* There must be a phone at Janet's house. But where were the girl's parents? *Didn't matter. Just get to Sidney. Get to the phone.*

She crawled on her belly those last few yards. "Sidney!" she yelled hoarsely. He didn't answer. She leaned over his cold body. "Oh, please, please don't be dead," she begged him. "Sidney, please! Can you hear me? No! This can't be happening!" His whole face was covered in sticky, near-frigid blood. She kissed his cold temple. His icy lips. "Don't go. Please come back to me. Sidney!"

His eyes fluttered open.

"Hang in there!" she croaked. "I'll get help."

He clutched at her hand and she pried his fingers away from her own. Half out of her mind, she made it to the house. No one answered the door. Thank the Goddess Sidney left the door unlocked. She stumbled through the dark living room, looking for a phone. There. On the little table. The phone! She grabbed the receiver and started to punch in 911, but her fingers cramped and she got it wrong. She tried again, her eyes drifting over the table. A lamp. A picture. She squinted, rubbing the blood from her eye with the back of her tattered sleeve.

Father and daughter.

Clarence and Janet.

A cold hand took the receiver from her blood-encrusted fingers. "I wouldn't do that, if I were you." It was Clarence. Bloody. Battered. But very alive and strong enough to be holding a knife at her throat. And wonder of wonders, he still wore a baseball cap, though half the side was ripped out. She swallowed hard, the blade of the knife nicking her Adam's apple. He reached over and tore the telephone cord out of the wall. "There's only one phone in the house. One line. We ain't rich, like other people.

"I tried to stop her," he said. "Really, I did. The Bindarts always treated me right. The girl was crazy. First the fire. Just to get attention. That's all it was. She spread them rumors among the others about the place being haunted. Wanted to keep people away from Tad. Such a friendly boy, he is. When that didn't work, Martha Owens disappeared." A sob hitched in his throat. "I was going to marry Martha. A real Pow-Wow, she was. A good woman. Didn't matter to me she was Mexican. I loved her just the same. But that Janet . . . oh . . . Janet. She claimed Martha got cold feet. Janet said she cashed in her savings bonds and gave the woman money to disappear. I believed her at first, but later on, I wasn't so sure. I tried to move her to a new school, thinking that would help. But it was too late, you see."

He shook his head and the knife trembled, cutting Bethany. She groaned in fear and pain. He released the pressure, but just a bit.

"I have to tell ya all this, because I have to kill ya. You made me hurt my little girl."

Bethany wanted to shake her head, but didn't dare. "No," she whispered. She felt so weak. If he didn't get it over with, she would collapse on the knife and do it for him. Her arms shook as she tried to put some weight on the small table. It wobbled dangerously.

"She got to stealing, did my little Janet. Just trinkets at first. She'd come home with all sorts of jewelry. Don't know where she got it from. Then Leslee Bindart caught her at the store, dipping in the till. That was it. My friendship with the family could only go so far. They fired her. What else could I do? I was trying to send her away to her momma, but the woman refused to take her at the last moment. Can't blame her. Janet is crazy.

"Alice came over here that Sunday. I'd just finished checking on Janet when the girl pulled up. She had the apple in her hand. I remember . . . " his voice drifted. "Janet must have put the poison in it. Couldn't be no other way."

Bethany made a silent entreaty the Mother. *Bring me strength. Bring me peace. And if I must die, please save Sidney.*

"My little girl is dead," said Clarence. "Gone to heaven, I expect."

"Maybe not," said Bethany, the table creaking as she tried to shift her weight. "Maybe we should call a doctor, an ambulance."

He shook his head. "No, I killed her. You know, Martha did so love my music."

He withdrew the knife from Bethany's throat just as the table collapsed under her weight. She rolled to the floor but he ignored her, shuffling through the living room and down a darkened hallway. She heard the snick of a door and the click of a lock. Bethany raised herself painfully to her knees, staring into the shadowed depth of the house, her breath rasping in her throat, her mouth hanging open.

Strains of fiddle music filtered around her as she stumbled into the night air. Carrying the dead phone receiver with her, she teetered out into the night, sinking beside Sidney's cold body, the music cloaking them with unending sadness.

She dropped the receiver by his side and knelt over him. Bethany stretched out stiff, swollen fingers, straining to capture the power. Tired. So tired. She held her hands over Sidney, hearing the slow beat of his heart in her soul, willing the energy of the universe to flow through her body and into his. They found her on top of him, fifteen minutes later, the raven perched on her motionless shoulder.

Chapter 18

The Salem house billowed with a multitude of voices mixed with the aroma of two turkeys and a large ham, along with all the savory smells of Thanksgiving fixings.

Ramona's place was set at one end of the snow-white tablecloth, Bethany's father at the other. Squished in between were all of the Bindarts, Tillie's family, Sidney and his father, Officer Charles, and Nam Chu dressed in flame-glo orange, her parents seated primly beside her, saying little and nodding a lot. They'd opted to leave the rest of the Chu clan at home. Mrs. Bindart scurried back and forth with Ramona between the dining room and the kitchen. Zee actually smiled, holding his two-year-old daughter on his lap, while Old Man Bindart recounted a hunting story. Cricket, pale but animated, sat next to her father, hanging on every word. Sidney, looking twice as haggard, held tightly to Bethany's hand. Officer Charles made goo-goo eyes at Ramona. Hecate sat in a corner, eyeing the turkey on the sideboard.

The families decided to wait until their children recovered, holding Thanksgiving at bay despite the practices of the rest of America, so that they could all celebrate together. Even Tad Bindart was well enough to join them. Bethany knew she looked as worn as the Bindart twins. Today was the first day she'd been allowed to get out of bed.

"Cricket," she said. "I'm dying to know. What happened?" As soon as it was out she realized her poor choice of words, but there was no taking them back now.

Old Man Bindart looked pained, but kept his mouth shut and nodded to Cricket.

"Janet came into the room that night. She was crazy. She tried to strangle me with a rope and when that didn't work, she tried to shove something down my throat. Everything fell into place, between her rantings and the process of elimination. During the summer Tad carried on with Janet and I guess she thought he was serious." She glanced at her father, but he didn't react.

Tad picked at the tablecloth with his uninjured hand. "You told me people would get hurt, but I didn't see how that was possible. I'm partly to blame for this whole mess. We weren't involved seriously. Just a little fun. I never dreamed she would think it was any more than that. We went to a couple of drive-ins, told each other ghost stories in the barn —kid stuff. She had a really vivid imagination and kept mixing reality with fantasy, so when I met

Alice, who was much more down-to-earth, I spent more time with her. I guess the problem started because I didn't realize that Janet was emotionally ill and I never thought about any sort of closure. I just dropped her."

Cricket took a drink from her water glass, then continued. "The more Tad distanced himself from Janet, the angrier she got. That's when she started messing around with magick, and she convinced Alice to do it with her. Alice went along because she thought that the tanglefoot, the Witch's ladder, and the love potion in the apple were so that Tad would find her more appealing, never realizing that Janet was trying to make Tad leave Alice and come back to her. The police think that's why Alice ate the apple. She thought she was consuming a love potion that would make her more desirable to Tad. There was something about it in the diary, but it was the last entry, and it was sketchy."

Officer Charles nodded.

"That Janet was one sick puppy," remarked Tillie.

"The police think that Janet tried to hurt me because, being Tad's twin, we've always been close. Tad must have talked about me a lot to Janet, and she saw me as a threat," said Cricket. "And the night I found the rabbit, Tad had been out with Alice. Janet must have seen them together and freaked out. We think the rabbit was meant for him, but we're really not sure."

Nam leaned forward. "What happened that night in your room?"

"I acted like I'd swallowed the poison, making strange sounds and keeling over. I was sure that Janet didn't really know how the poison worked, because I remember the police telling my father that Alice died at home, alone, which means that Alice didn't eat the apple at Janet's house. After Janet left the room, I ran to the window and watched her cross the parking lot. I was sure she was headed for her own house. I ran into Clarence at the top of the stairs and told him about Janet. He must have known something bad might happen, because he was frantic looking for her."

Bethany's hand flew to her lips. "Cricket! He could have killed you!"

"He just pushed me aside and I fell down the stairs. He didn't even seem to notice. He rushed down the stairs like I didn't exist. The fall made me silly in the head. Dad found me not too long after that, but it took awhile for me to come around, and when I did, I wasn't making any sense. Clarence was long gone by then. Dad tried to call the police, but someone cut the phone lines into the house and the store. Sidney's dad was still around and he used his cell phone. That's how we finally got in touch with the authorities, except they didn't know about Janet, only Clarence. I passed out before I could tell Daddy that part." She looked sheepish. "I guess I wasn't making much sense."

Old Man Bindart and Sidney's father nodded in unison.

"But where was the Bronco?" asked Sidney.

"I can answer that," said Tillie. "Nam and I found it in that fancy barn."

"Yes," said Old Man Bindart. "I had no idea the police were looking for it. I knew it was there all along. When Clarence bought it he asked me not to say anything to the migrant workers. He didn't want it stolen, and he didn't want people asking where he got the money for it. Clarence had been saving for a lot of years, and I knew he paid for the vehicle fair and square. He bought it when the weather turned cold and used the back road to drive in and out of the property."

"What happened at the barn, Tillie?" asked Nam.

"Clarence came tearing in, opened up the big doors, and roared out of there. Just about ran Nam over. We tried to follow as fast as we could, but we were on foot. By the time we reached the parking lot, all heck was breaking loose, cop cars everywhere. It took a while for us to get to Mr. Bindart. People heard the Bronco crash, but with the open fields, we couldn't be sure which direction the sound came from. When we told them where you both went, they zoomed down the road to make sure you were okay. Nam and I followed in the Toyota."

Old Man Bindart took up the story. "We saw the wrecked Bronco first, and found Janet. Poor girl.

We probably wouldn't have gotten to you as quickly as we did if not for that bird." He jerked his thumb over to the large cage hanging between the dining room and living room. The raven cocked his head, staring at all of them.

"That crazy bird kept flapping around our heads, and then flying off. Circling again, and zipping away. It was Tillie that done followed the bird and found you two," he said, looking at Bethany and Sidney. "Good thing she did, too!"

"And what about Clarence?" asked Bethany.

The table grew silent. "Oh, honey," said Bethany's father. "He must have passed away not long after he let you go. We found him in his room, holding his fiddle."

"But I heard him play the music . . . I heard it for a long time."

Carl Salem looked extremely uncomfortable. "According to the county coroner, as soon as he sat down, the severity of his injuries would have killed him instantaneously. Besides, Officer Charles saw the body himself as well as the contents of the room. There were no strings in the fiddle."

"None?" whispered Bethany.

Officer Charles coughed. "Not a one."

The room was incredibly quiet. Even the bird remained mute. The only audible sound came from the grandfather clock in the hallway.

Bethany took a deep breath. "Last question. Who hit my car?"

Officer Charles spoke up. "I can answer that. It appears that Janet was following you. She thought you were getting too close. She hit your car using her father's Bronco."

"But we didn't know anything!" exclaimed Nam.

Officer Charles shook his head. "Didn't matter what you did or didn't know, the girl thought you had information that could damage her. We have eyewitness accounts that put a young lady behind the wheel of that Bronco. We also know that she took the chinchilla rabbits from the agricultural room at your school."

"But what about all the damage to the farm equipment?" asked Sidney.

"I can answer that," replied Leslee. "Alice was responsible."

"Alice!" cried the girls.

"She thought that if she sabotaged the farm, it would ultimately help Tad escape our father's unreasonable rules." She looked guiltily down at the tablecloth, avoiding her father's gaze.

Officer Charles nodded his head. "It was in her diary."

Old Man Bindart spoke up. "It was really all my fault, now that we seem to be passing the blame around," he looked at Tad. "I was so afraid for you children that I stopped being human. I let my fear dictate my actions. Leslee," he turned to his eldest daughter. "I humbly apologize for any pain I've caused you. You stood by this family through thick and thin. I can't believe I was such an ass."

Mrs. Bindart clapped her hands. "Here, here!"

A lone tear dripped down Leslee's cheek.

"And Tad?" said Mr. Bindart. "You and I have to talk about that computer you want, and if you two are interested in public school, I guess I can stomach a whirl if you can."

Tad and Cricket exchanged glances, but it was Tad who spoke. "I'd really like that computer, sir, but I can wait until we get the farm back on its feet. As for public school, Cricket and I may decide to go, but for now, we'd like to continue schooling at home. Zee has offered to help us."

Old Man Bindart cleared his throat. "Zee?"

All eyes riveted to the burly fellow near the other end of the table.

"Welcome to the family!"

The group broke into several conversations at once. Ramona tapped on the crystal goblet with a fork. "Attention, attention! Reverend Alexander will give the grace."

Tillie's father stood, smiling eloquently around the table. "It has always been my desire that folks of different faiths can gather together to share a meal, and think as one for the good of all." He winked at Ramona. "Could we join hands today, to say the blessing."

The raven squawked and ruffled his feathers.

"I tried to let him go," said Ramona. "But he refuses to budge. I can't let him fly all over the house, so he's got to stay in the cage, especially with food on the table!"

"We begin with a circle of prayer," boomed Reverend Alexander's voice through the room. "A circle that is without beginning, and unending, as the cycle of life moves from birth, to death, to rebirth. In these few weeks before the holiday, we have seen both the cycle of death, and the cycle of birth." He smiled at Leslee Bindart. She smiled back and lowered her head. "We have lost family, and we have found them again. We have risen from our hatred, our fear, and our pain into, hopefully, a sincere wish to live in harmony and help our fellow human. For some, our most precious commodity, our children, might have been lost to us forever, but through the graciousness of Spirit, through the courage of these same children, in togetherness we share the bounty of the earth now set before us."

Hecate edged closer to the sideboard.

"And we are thankful."

"Amen!" chorused many. "So mote it be!" said the Witches.

Hecate dive-bombed the turkey, sending the twenty-four-pound bird wheeling into the air, the carcass exploding on the beige carpet. Bits of stuffing dripped off the wall, leaving greasy trails in their wake. Ramona squealed something unintelligible and ran for her broom. Hecate pounced on the bird, claws extended, kitty incisors going in for the gusto.

Carl Salem cleared his throat. "I guess we should have given him a plate of his own."

Everyone burst into laugher as they watched Ramona try to pry the cat off the turkey with her broom, squawking in French, eyes rolling in supplication.

Bethany excused herself from the table and retrieved Nam's jewelry from her room. When she returned everyone was busy eating, laughing, and talking about every subject but the recent events. Neither Hecate nor the deceased turkey remained to be seen. Quietly, so as not to be overheard by the others, she handed the jewelry over to Nam, saying, "I sort of retrieved these for you. I think Janet took some of them, and I'm afraid the bird might have taken the others. I can't be sure. Birds like shiny things, you know."

Nam smiled gratefully, putting her WNO necklace on first, clutching it to her heart. "I'm sorry it was your turn to get beat up," Nam said, her orange-glo lips downturned.

Tillie elbowed Nam. "She didn't mean it that way," said Tillie. "It's just that Nam got the short end of the stick last time."

Bethany nodded. "No offense taken."

Ramona served seven different pies, three kinds of ice cream, and two cakes for dessert. The conversation died to pleased groaning over full stomachs. Slowly, the guests left for home. Cricket stopped on the way out, speaking to Bethany in an excited whisper. "Everything is working out! Sidney's father remade the loan on the farm and lowered the payments. We're going to run hayrides through December, maybe even do something for Christmas. My father is talking about opening up a haunted house next year in the barn, just like Granddad used to do. And get a load of this! My sister is pregnant, and she's been married to Zee for over five years. Can you believe that? And Zee's a famous children's book author!" Bethany looked at the solemn Zee. "You're kidding."

"Ever hear of Zeddadiah Linquist?"

"Sure."

"That's Zee!" Cricket turned to go, but there was something Bethany really wanted to know. "Look, I know it's none of my business, but did Tad really . . . you know . . . love Alice?"

A sad smile crept over Cricket's face. "He showed me a bracelet he was going to give her for Christmas. It was engraved, 'I will love you forever.'" It just goes to show that beauty is only skin deep. He thought the world of her." She gave Bethany a big hug.

Sidney remained behind, cuddling with Bethany on the family room sofa. He leaned over to kiss Bethany and they both groaned from full stomachs. "How are you feeling?" asked Bethany.

"Like someone beat the tar out of me with a shovel," he said.

Bethany's father started a fire in the fireplace and retreated to the dining room for more pie. They both stared into the crackling flames. Hecate lay indolently at the other end of the sofa, extended belly positioned to soak up the warmth of the fire, tail occasionally flicking in kitty sleep. He was probably dreaming of snacking on the raven still perched in the dining room cage. Perhaps for dessert? She'd have to do something about that bird. Had it been Janet's pet? She would never know. Hecate began to snore.

"I feel like you're beating yourself up over something," said Sidney quietly. "Want to share?"

Bethany moved her head. Her shoulder still ached. Sharing was not an easy task for a Scorpio, but she might as well give it a shot. "I should have known that Janet was practicing magick, but it just never dawned on me."

"And how would you know that?"

"Magickal people just know. I should have seen it, but I was so worried about my own life that I didn't notice."

"Bethany, there are over a thousand kids in our school. How could you have known?"

She remained silent.

"I thought as much. Tillie and Nam don't know, do they?"

Bethany could feel her heart thumping.

"That you're a hereditary Witch. That your mother was practicing and her mother before her. That it's in your blood and not from books."

"You can't ever tell them," said Bethany. "Then they would feel we're not the same, but we are the same. I know that in my heart. Whether your parents were of the Old Religion or you picked the faith up on your own, the Goddess calls us all equally to Her service. Promise me you won't say anything."

"I promise." He slightly shifted his legs. "Bethany, I need to tell you something."

"I hope it's not about my mother. I'm not ready for that," said Bethany.

"No, actually, it's about Martha Owens, the migrant worker."

"Oh. Well. Do I really want to hear this?"

Sidney took a deep breath. It hitched in his chest, and he moaned.

"Do you want me to move?" asked Bethany.

"Not on your life," he said, holding her firmly.

"All right. What about Martha?"

"She's buried in the butterfly garden."

"The what?"

"It's the garden beside the store. They grow special flowers. In the spring and summer, the garden is filled with butterflies. She says she always loved watching the garden. It was so peaceful. She wants to stay there."

"She told you this?"

"Yes."

"When?"

"When I was half unconscious, waiting for help to come. She sat with me awhile. She told me I would be okay. That I would pull through, and that when you came back to try to help me that you weren't strong enough to do it alone. I should help by allowing your energy to flow through me. I should look into your soul and ride with the intensity. That I wasn't to be afraid."

"And did you look into my soul?"

"Down to your toes."

Bethany moved a bit, stretching for comfort. She didn't quite know if she liked anyone looking into her private self.

"I told her I wouldn't say anything. That I would let her stay there. But I wanted you to know."

The fire popped and snapped, the walls filled with soft, dancing light. Bethany snuggled back into Sidney's arms and yawned.

"There's something I've been meaning to ask you," said Bethany.

"Shoot."

"Did you really sign up for the wrestling team?"

"And what if I did? You think I couldn't make it?"

She grinned. "I'm dating a jock. I don't believe it." She kissed his cheek and he sighed.

In the distance, just beyond the window, the merry sound of a fiddle nestled against the glass, seeping in through the sill, waltzing across the room, tickling their ears. The little hairs on Bethany's arms stood at attention. "Do you hear that?" she whispered.

Sidney nodded, his face a mysterious mask of light and shadow.

Hecate yawned, one eye popping open, then the other. The cat began batting at the air, as if playing with a string dangled by an unseen hand, his claws extended and glittering in the half-light.

Bethany and Sidney looked with disbelief at the shadows cavorting across the family room walls.

Specters . . .

. . . mimicking the silhouettes . . .

. . . of frolicking rabbits.

The music died. The room grew frigid, and the momentary peaceful feeling that they had both shared seeing the affirmation of the Goddess was extinguished in a millisecond. Bethany's heart felt like it was pumping ice water. In the dining room, the raven began to squawk and screech. They could hear Ramona fussing at him in French followed by the low murmuring of her father as he tried to calm the bird. The flames in the fireplace guttered and died, leaving only glowing embers behind.

Sidney gripped Bethany's shoulders. "What is the fastest conjuration of protection that you know?" he asked her tightly.

"'I walk through circles of light that none may pass nor harm me,'" replied Bethany. "Why?"

They could hear the raven rattling his cage.

"Because we are about to have a little visitation," whispered Sidney. "Where there's order, chaos will follow. You can't have one without the other, and I think you are going to experience . . . the other. Just remember, even though you can't see her, your mother is with you."

Hecate flipped over and backed against the sofa, his ears flat, his fangs revealed, a long hiss escaping from his throat.

New shadows slid down the wall, moving rapidly to the middle of the floor, coalescing in a murky puddle of undulating blackness. The room filled with a horrible stench.

"Oh!" cried Bethany. "What is that smell?"

The phantom rose, a long arm extended, its head crooked and bent.

"Janet!" cried Bethany. Sidney tried to jump forward to protect her, but his injuries slowed him down. Bethany was already on her feet, pushing him back, facing the demented creature alone, her heart pounding in her chest, her breath fast and frightened. "This is between us," said Bethany through clenched teeth, staring at the evil that was once a girl named Janet. Bethany realized that she had no tools, only that of her own true self.

She gulped furiously, her skin growing clammy. For a moment she felt a strange sensation of disembodiment, her mind grasping for the right thing to do. Nauseating spurts of adrenaline chugged through her veins as the monstrous evil crept toward her. Think. *Think!*

When she was little, her mother taught her a conjuration set to verse by Doreen Valiente, one of the most famous English Witches of the twentieth century. Her mind faltered, tripping over the first words. *How did it start!* "Great Mother, help me now," she whispered, desperately seeking the words.

She raised her chin in defiance, pulling on every bit of energy she could muster. From within and from without, she tugged that essence, balling her hands into fists with the effort.

The words! What were the words!

And then they came to her. In bits at first, then flowing from her whole being. "Darksome night and shining moon," she began. "Hearken to the Witches' Rune!" Her voice grew stronger "East and West, South and North, hear me now, I call ye forth!"

Janet wavered, her eyes roving in her head. "You're dead, Bethany Salem," she rasped, moving forward.

"By all the powers of land and sea, be obedient unto me!" screamed Bethany.

The drapes at the windows began to sway as a sharp wind shot through the room, fanning the embers in the fireplace to bright orange. Deadly hot ashes and flammable, spiraling sparks whooshed against the grate.

Bethany didn't stop. "Wand and pentacle, cup and sword, waken ye unto my word! Cord and censor, totem and knife, waken all ye into life!" Bethany stretched out her arms as if gathering in the power. She could feel the energy begin to course through her body, rippling across her arms, pulsing through the arteries of her heart.

Janet took a step closer, drooling, smiling. "I'm taking you with me, Bethany. Prepare to die tonight!"

Slowly, Bethany began to raise her arms. "By all the powers of the Witch's blade, come ye now as the charge is made! Queen of Heaven, Queen of Hel, grant your aid unto this spell. Horned Hunter of the night, work my will with all your might!" Bethany's arms were straight up in the air now, the power blasting through her body as she looked heavenward, her fingers splayed toward the ceiling.

Janet cringed, stumbled, but continued to reach for Bethany, her rotting arms growing longer, nails clawing toward Bethany's face.

"By all the powers of land and sea, as I will, so mote it be! By all the might of moon and sun, as I say it shall be done!"

Flames burst from the logs in the fireplace, lighting the room in orange glow, the heat sizzling Janet's skin as she thrust herself toward Bethany. Bethany clapped her hands three times, screaming, "Begone! Back to the grave! And may the Goddess have mercy on your miserable soul!"

The raven screamed. A horrible crash, and the next moment the room was filled with beating wings and raven shrieks. The bird dove for Janet's heart, its beak piercing through her chest, flying straight into her blackened soul, her blood-curdling shrieks echoing through the room as her essence burst apart, scattering shafts of skittering light that rebounded off the walls in a giant thunderclap.

Slowly, Bethany lowered her arms, staring at the empty air, the breath rasping in her throat, her heart pounding in her chest, her blood banging in her ears. A lone coal-black feather drifted past her cheek and settled on the carpet at her feet. Hecate, whiskers twitching, poked his nose out from under the sofa.

"Coward," Bethany said.

Ramona rushed into the family room, broom in hand, with Carl Salem close behind her.

Bethany turned to them, brushing her hands together several times. "And that takes care of *that!*" Bethany said forcefully as the two stared at her with mouths agape. "One thing I cannot abide is a murderess who refuses to stay dead!"

"'Atta girl!" exclaimed Sidney.

Her father stepped forward, his brow crinkled in a quizzical frown. "What murderess? Bethany, is your fever coming back? What happened to the bird?"

Bethany pointed to the window, where a raven sat patiently, peering in at them through the glass. He tapped three times on the pane, then disappeared into the night. "Oh," said Bethany, winking at Ramona, "he was just a temporary house guest."

Carl Salem put his hands on his hips. "By the way, young lady, we need to talk about your car and how you'll be handling your finances in the future. We must also discuss this penchant of yours for solving true crimes."

The housekeeper, eyes wide, said, "Ramona thinks she will go light a candle."

Epilogue

Ramona's House-Cleansing Spell

In this story Ramona, the magickal housekeeper, uses an old folk spell to cleanse the Salem house of negative energies. She uses an onion in the story, but you can also use yarn. Here's how to do it:

Supplies: You will need a skein of red yarn, your favorite incense, a piece of paper, a black marker, a broom, and a rubber band.

Instructions: Pass the skein of yarn through the smoke of your favorite incense to cleanse the yarn and state its purpose, that of cleansing your home of negative energies. Roll the skein of red yarn into a ball. This may take a while, but it's worth it. As you are rolling the yarn into a ball, think of it as a magickal vacuum cleaner that will collect any negative energy like a magnet. Once you have finished with the yarn, write the following spell on the piece of paper:

Magick broom be true to me
Sweep away negativity.
In its place leave peace and love
With Goddess blessings from above.

Draw an equal-armed cross (+) on the back of the paper to seal the spell. Wrap the paper around the broom handle. Secure with the rubber band. Sweep out the entire house, pushing the ball of yarn around every room with the broom. When you are finished, sweep the yarn outside and off your property. You now have one of three options:

1. If your parents approve and you are careful, burn the ball of yarn. (I warn you, it will smell.)

2. Bury the yarn off your property.

3. Throw it in the trash off your property.

Dispose of the paper in the same manner.

This spell carries extra power on a Saturday (a banishing day), or during the waning moon.

NATIONAL HOTLINES

The following numbers were collected by a Pennsylvania sheriff (a friend of mine) in case you ever need them. Don't be shy. If you need help, please call. If you have to do a report in school on any of the issues listed below, the people at these numbers will be happy to supply you with information.

Alcohol and Drug Abuse

Al-Anon & Alateen: 1-800-356-9996

National Clearinghouse for Alcohol & Drug Information: 1-800-SAY-NOTO

National Cocaine Hotline: 1-800-262-2463

Alcohol & Drug Dependency Hopeline: 1-800-622-2255

National Institute on Drug Abuse Hotline: 1-800-622-HELP

Mothers Against Drunk Driving: 1-800-438-MADD

Abuse

Bureau of Indian Affairs Child Abuse Hotline: 1-800-633-5133

Boy's Town: 1-800-448-3000

Child Help USA: 1-800-422-4453

National Respite Locators Service: 1-800-773-5433

National Domestic Violence Hotline:
1-800-799-7233

National Clearinghouse of Child Abuse and
Neglect: 1-800-394-3366

National Resource Center on Domestic Violence:
1-800-553-2508

Rape, Abuse & Incest National Network:
1-800-656-4673

Resource Center on Domestic Violence, Child
Protection and Custody: 1-800-527-3223

Runaway Hotlines

Covenant House Nineline: 1-800-999-9999

National Runaway Switchboard: 1-800-621-4000

National Child Welfare

Child Find of America: 1-800-I-AM-LOST

Child Quest International Sighting Line:
1-800-248-8020

National Referral Network for Kids in Crisis:
1-800-KID-SAVE

Health & AIDS/HIV

AIDS Helpline: 1-800-548-4659

Ask A Nurse Connection: 1-800-535-1111

National AIDS Hotline: 1-800-342-AIDS

STD National Hotline: 1-800-227-8922

About Silver

Silver RavenWolf is the author of over sixteen how-to and fictional books relating to the application of the magickal sciences. She resides in south-central Pennsylvania with her husband of twenty-one years, four children, sheltie, and pet rat. Her primary interests are divinatory tools, astrology, hypnotherapy, reading, swimming, and getting through life in a positive and productive way. To read about Silver, her touring schedule, upcoming events, and books, visit Silver's website at:

http://www.silverravenwolf.com

To Write to Silver

If you wish to contact the author or would like more information about this book, please write to:

Silver RavenWolf
℅ Llewellyn Worldwide
P.O. Box 64383, Dept. 0-7387-0049-5
St. Paul, MN 55164-0383, U.S.A.

Please enclose a self-addressed stamped envelope for reply, or $1.00 to cover costs. If outside U.S.A., enclose international postal reply coupon.

About the Series

In September of 1998 my book titled *Teen Witch* was published, shocking myself and the publishing world with phenomenal sales (142,037 copies sold to date). I wrote the book because I cared about kids and I wanted them to have legitimate information on how to work real magick. I hung the rave reviews and the advertising poster given to me by Llewellyn above my desk. For me, it was a dream come true. I'd written a book that would make a difference in people's lives. While working on other projects, I would stare at that poster, thinking about the thousands of teens reading my book.

One afternoon, my sixteen-year-old daughter, Falcon, caught me at my desk once again mesmerized by that poster. "Too bad those kids on the cover of your book aren't real," she said. "I mean, they look like real people, don't they?"

The hairs on the back of my neck stood up as I continued to look at the poster. "Yeah," I breathed. "I've stared at this picture so long, they *do* seem like they are more than just a book cover. It's like . . . I don't know . . . as if I've known them all along. That one's Bethany," I said, pointing to the dark-haired girl in the center of the picture. "And I think the African-American girl looks just like a Tillie. What do you think?"

Falcon surveyed the poster, then turned to me with a sly smile. "You know, Echo is always complaining that you never wrote fiction for us." Echo is Falcon's older sister. "Why don't you write a story about the kids on the poster?"

And that's how the Witches' Night Out *Witches' Chillers* series was born. Although the story is entirely fictional, I set about to devise a world where the teens use real magick, not the fairy-tale stuff. It wasn't easy. In the world of fiction, anything can happen. It would have been so easy to give Bethany and her friends super-powers, but I know that real magick doesn't work that way. Conjuring magick is a skill that one acquires after hard work and practice. It takes longer than a snap of your fingers, and it almost never happens with the bells and whistles of a Hollywood film—but it does happen. Bethany and her friends are students of magick, which in a way makes it all the more fun! They will make mistakes as they wrestle with school, family problems, and relationships with peers—not to mention the pain of dealing with a job at the same time, an already rocky road for any kid. Throw in the desire to solve crimes, and the characters become people like you or me. That's why their world is such an interesting one!

Because . . . it *could* be real.

☽ REACH FOR THE MOON

Llewellyn publishes hundreds of books on your favorite subjects!
To get these exciting books, including the ones on the following pages,
check your local bookstore or order them directly from Llewellyn.

Order by Phone
- Call toll-free within the U.S. and Canada, 1-800-THE MOON
- In Minnesota, call (651) 291-1970
- We accept VISA, MasterCard, and American Express

Order by Mail
- Send the full price of your order (MN residents add 7% sales tax)
  in U.S. funds, plus postage & handling to:
  Llewellyn Worldwide
  P.O. Box 64383, Dept. 0-7387-0049-5
  St. Paul, MN 55164–0383, U.S.A.

Postage & Handling
- **Standard** (U.S., Mexico, & Canada). If your order is:
  $20.00 or under, add $5.00
  $20.01–$100.00, add $6.00
  Over $100, shipping is free
(Continental U.S. orders ship UPS. AK, HI, PR, & P.O. Boxes ship USPS 1st
class. Mex. & Can. ship PMB.)
- **Second Day Air** (Continental U.S. only): $10.00 for one book + $1.00
per each additional book
- **Express** (AK, HI, & PR only) [Not available for P.O. Box delivery. For
street address delivery only.]: $15.00 for one book + $1.00 per each
additional book
- **International Surface Mail:** Add $1.00 per item
- **International Airmail:** Books—Add the retail price of each item;
Non-book items—Add $5.00 per item

Please allow 4–6 weeks for delivery on all orders.
Postage and handling rates subject to change.

Discounts
We offer a 20% discount to group leaders or
agents. You must order a minimum of 5 copies of
the same book to get our special quantity price.

FREE CATALOG
Get a free copy of our color catalog, *New Worlds of
Mind and Spirit.* Subscribe for just $10.00 in the
United States and Canada ($30.00 overseas, airmail).
Many bookstores carry *New Worlds*—ask for it!

Visit our website at www.llewellyn.com for more information.

Teen Witch Kit: Everything You Need to Make Magick!

Silver RavenWolf

Here is everything the novice spell-caster needs to practice the Craft of the Wise—and be a force for good. Step into the sacred space and discover the secrets of one of the world's oldest mysteries: the art and science of white magick, a gentle, loving practice. The kit contains a beautifully illustrated book of instruction, plus six magickal talismans, salt, and a spell bag. The kit box converts into your own personal altar.

Silver RavenWolf, one of today's most famous Witches and author of the best-selling *Teen Witch*, provides the quick-reading guidebook, complete with instructions on how to prepare yourself for magick, create a sacred space, call up the spirit, and draw down the Moon.

All the spells are tailored to 13- to 18-year olds, and can be cast using the items in the kit and common objects found around the house. It's easy to follow the step-by-step instructions and clear magickal symbols. There is even a section on how to write your own spells. The book also reveals the white magick code of honor, and includes a glossary of terms, a suggested reading list, and a guide to the top magickal Internet sites.

1-56718-554-1 $24.95
7½ x 7½ **boxed kit contains:**
  128-pp. illus. book • spell bag • spell salt • golden coin • silver wish cord • silver bell • natural quartz crystal • silver pentacle pendant • yes/no coin

Teen Witch: Wicca for a New Generation

Silver RavenWolf

Teenagers and young adults comprise a growing market for books on Witchcraft and magick, yet there has never been a book written specifically for the teen seeker. Now, Silver RavenWolf, one of the most well-known Wiccans today and the mother of four young Witches, gives teens their own handbook on what it takes and what it means to be a Witch. Humorous and compassionate, *Teen Witch* gives practical advice for dealing with everyday life in a magickal way. From homework and crabby teachers to parents and dating, this book guides teens through the ups and downs of life as they move into adulthood. Spells are provided that address their specific concerns, such as the "Call Me Spell" and "The Exam Spell."

Parents will also find this book informative and useful as a discussion tool with their children. Discover the beliefs of Witchcraft, Wiccan traditions, symbols, holidays, rituals, and more.

1-56718-725-0
288 pp., 7 x 10   **$12.95**

Witches' Night Out
(Witches' Chillers #1)
Silver RavenWolf

Now, from the author of *Teen Witch*—the wildly popular guide to Witchcraft—comes the first in a new series of spellbinders written specifically for teens. Featuring the five characters on the cover of *Teen Witch*, these fictional books will focus on the strength, courage, and willpower of the teens to overcome seemingly insurmountable obstacles, with enough authentic magickal practice thrown in to keep you on the edge of your seat. Every book features a spell that readers can do themselves.

Main character Bethany Salem, 16, is on her own most of the time. Five years ago her mother died, leaving her in the care of her father, a New York City cop, who has deposited her in the suburbs with their Santerían housekeeper.

The adventure begins when enterprising Bethany starts a coven with her friends. In *Witches' Night Out*, the teens find themselves sleuthing to determine who caused the fatal automobile wreck of their friend Joe.

1-56718-728-5
240 pp., 4⅛ x 6¾ $4.99

Witches' Night of Fear
(Witches' Chillers #2)
Silver RavenWolf

In the first book, *Witches' Night Out*, the teens find themselves sleuthing to determine the cause of the fatal car crash of a friend. Now, in *Witches' Night of Fear*, they are pulled into a local homicide of a convenience store clerk and an active case in New York City.

> *A shadow darted out from underneath the direction of the willow tree, sending a thrill of fear up her spine. Had someone seen her? Magick done in front of non-believers lost some, if not all, of its power. Bethany backed up to slam the window shut, but the wind caught her hair and whipped the ends in her eyes, making her hesitate. In that split second a black, gloved hand reached out from the darkness beyond the window and grabbed her by the throat. She couldn't see the face . . .*

1-56718-718-8
368 pp., 4³⁄₁₆ x 6⁷⁄₈   **$5.99**

Wild Girls
*The Path of the
Young Goddess*

Patricia Monaghan

Maiden, Mother, Crone. Of the three faces of the goddess, the maiden corresponds to the part of a woman's soul that is always questing, always free to move and explore, always free to follow her own heart. She is among the most loving and giving—and heroic—of the goddess images.

She is the Wild Girl. Like natural wilderness, she lives by her own laws. And she is part of all women—from preteens who are just beginning their path to the goddess, to adults who want to re-connect with the passionate girl they once were.

The stories in this book represent some of the many visions of the Wild Girl found throughout the world. Each story is followed by commentary and activities such as building an altar, creating healing rituals, and working with dreams. You will also learn how to start your own Wild Girls' Circle.

1-56718-442-1
240 pp., 7½ x 9⅛, illus. $14.95

To order, call 1-800-THE MOON
Prices subject to change without notice

Angels

Silver RavenWolf

Angels do exist. Here, in this complete text, you will find practical information on how to invite these angelic beings into your life. Build an angelic altar . . . meet the archangels in meditation . . . contact your guardian angel . . . create angel sigils and talismans . . . work magick with the Angelic Rosary . . . talk to the deceased. You will learn to work with angels to gain personal insights and assist in the healing of the planet as well as yourself.

Angels do not belong to any particular religious structure—they are universal and open their arms to humans of all faiths, bringing love and power into people's lives.

1-56718-724-2
288 pp., 7 x 10, illus.   **$14.95**

Silver's Spells for Prosperity
Silver RavenWolf

Take charge of your finances the Silver way! Now one of the most famous Witches in the world today shows you how to get the upper hand on your cash flow with techniques personally designed and tested by the author herself. She will show you how to banish those awful old debts without heartache, get money back from someone who owes you, and transform your money energy so it flows in the ~~the~~ right direction—toward you! An abundance of spells can aid you in everything from winning a court case to getting creditors off your back. You'll also find a wealth of historical and practical information on spell elements and ingredients.

Silver's Spells for Prosperity is the first in a new series of five books by best-selling Wiccan author Silver RavenWolf.

1-56718-726-9
240 pp., 5³⁄₁₆ x 6, illus.   **$7.95**

Silver's Spells for Protection

Silver RavenWolf

What do you do when you discover that your best friend at work sabotaged your promotion? Or if a neighbor suddenly decides that you don't belong in his town? What if a group of teens sets out to make your life a living hell? What if . . . *Silver's Spells for Protection* contains tips for dealing with all these situations, and more.

This book covers how to handle stalkers, abusers, and other nasties with practical information as well as magickal techniques. It also covers some of the smaller irritants in life—like protecting yourself from your mother-in-law's caustic tongue and how to avoid that guy who's out to take your job from you.

Silver's Spells for Protection is the second in a new series of five books by best-selling Wiccan author Silver RavenWolf.

1-56718-729-3
264 pp., 5³⁄₁₆ x 6, illus.   **$7.95**

Silver's Spells for Love
Silver RavenWolf

Does your current relationship need a spicy boost? Have you been browsing for love in all the wrong places? Maybe you want to conceive a magickal baby? From finding a new lover to handling that couch potato partner, *Silver's Spells for Love* has more than 100 ideas, potions, and incantations to bring titillating passion into your waiting arms. Whether you want affection, commitment, or a hot time on the town tonight, this book will teach you the nuances of spellcasting for love!

- Prepare incenses, oils, and powders for love
- Learn how to wisely draw a lover toward you
- Boost the passion in your current relationship
- Make the right moves when good love goes bad

… and learn dozens of ways to tap into that universal energy called love!

1-56718-552-5
312 pp., 5³⁄₁₆ x 6, illus.   **$7.95**